'I'd like [s...]

He reached [out ... her] hand. When he pulled her glove off it felt as if he was undressing her. He laid his gentle fingers around hers, and it was as if they were naked already. Neve leaned forward, brushing her lips against his.

The suddenness of his next move activated his seat belt, and for a moment he was pinned against the seat. Cursing, he punched the release, twisting round and pulling her into his arms. Sudden heat jolted through her when he kissed her.

'Come inside.'

The gear-shift was in the way, and the steering wheel wouldn't allow him to get as close as she'd like. Their *clothes* wouldn't allow him to get as close as she'd like...

'If I let you go...?'

'You're going to have to. One step back and two steps forward.'

His [...] way you [...]

Dear Reader

When I was writing my first book, one of the (many) details I worried about was the fact that I'd described a very sharp frost and frozen pipes before Christmas. Would this be entirely believable? In the previous few years we'd had mild winters, without any really cold weather before Christmas. But the unpredictable British climate came to my rescue, and December 2010—the winter before that first book was published—was one of the coldest we'd experienced for a hundred years, with enough snow to make my December cold snap seem a little bit understated!

So this time around I've no qualms about giving my characters something a bit more extreme to deal with. Dr Neve Harrison doesn't have the luxury of being able to give in to adverse weather conditions. She's struggling to get to all her patients, despite heavy snow and blocked roads. So when Joe Lamont turns up on her doorstep, ready and able to help, it seems that her luck has changed.

Together, they're more than a match for those adverse weather conditions—but Joe himself is a more daunting proposition. His secrets threaten to break Neve's heart, and deprive her of the thing she wants most in the world.

I hope you enjoy Joe and Neve's story. I'm always thrilled to hear from readers, and you can contact me via my website at www.annieclaydon.com

Annie x

SNOWBOUND WITH THE SURGEON

BY
ANNIE CLAYDON

Published in Great Britain 2014
by Mills & Boon, an imprint of Harlequin (UK) Limited,
Eton House, 18-24 Paradise Road, Richmond, Surrey, TW9 1SR

© 2014 Annie Claydon

ISBN: 978-0-263-90808-4

Harlequin (UK) Limited's policy is to use papers that are natural,
renewable and recyclable products and made from wood grown in
sustainable forests. The logging and manufacturing processes conform
to the legal environmental regulations of the country of origin.

Printed and bound in Spain
by Blackprint CPI, Barcelona

Cursed from an early age with a poor sense of direction and a propensity to read, **Annie Claydon** spent much of her childhood lost in books. After completing her degree in English Literature she indulged her love of romantic fiction and spent a long, hot summer writing a book of her own. It was duly rejected and life took over. A series of U-turns led in the unlikely direction of a career in computing and information technology, but the lure of the printed page proved too much to bear, and she now has the perfect outlet for the stories which have always run through her head, writing Medical Romance™ for Mills & Boon®. Living in London—a city where getting lost can be a joy—she has no regrets for having taken her time in working her way back to the place that she started from.

Recent titles by Annie Claydon:

A DOCTOR TO HEAL HER HEART
200 HARLEY STREET: THE ENIGMATIC SURGEON
ONCE UPON A CHRISTMAS NIGHT…
RE-AWAKENING HIS SHY NURSE
THE REBEL AND MISS JONES
THE DOCTOR MEETS HER MATCH
DOCTOR ON HER DOORSTEP
ALL SHE WANTS FOR CHRISTMAS

These and other titles are also available in eBook format
from www.millsandboon.co.uk

Dedication

To Noreen, who taught me how to end well.

Praise for
Annie Claydon:

CHAPTER ONE

THIRTY PACES TO her gate. Neve counted them all. After that, ten paces would be enough to take her up the front path. It turned out to be eleven because she slipped on the ice, grabbing at the porch rails to steady herself and wrenching her shoulder as her heavy medical bag fell to the ground.

She waved her hand in front of the sensor for the porch light, and nothing happened. The electricity was still off, then. All the same, the cast-iron stove in the kitchen would be throwing out heat, and she couldn't wait to get inside. Just as she was about to savour the moment of sliding the key into the lock of her own front door, her phone rang. Dammit. If she had to go out in the snow again tonight…

If she had to go out again tonight, then so be it. She'd turn around, slide back down the front path and hope that it wouldn't take twenty minutes to start her car this time. The vision of sipping a hot drink and letting her toes thaw in front of the stove, which had carried her through the last hours of a very long day, began to recede.

'Yeah, Maisie. What have you got for me?'

'Good news…'

'Really?' Neve took the risk of further disappointment and opened the front door, stepping inside and dumping her bag in the hallway. It wasn't much warmer in here, but the kitchen door was closed against the chill in the rest of the old farmhouse. 'Is it safe to take my coat off?'

'Aren't you home yet?'

'Just. It took me over an hour to get back from my last appointment. The road through Cryersbridge was blocked by a car that slid out of control, and we had to wait until it was towed.'

'You must be frozen. Are you in the warm now, pet?' Maisie Johnstone was the wife of the senior partner of the Yorkshire practice that Neve had joined eighteen months ago, and sometimes took it upon herself to mother Neve. That was okay. Neve could do with a bit of that at the moment.

'Hold on…' Neve tramped through to the kitchen, her boots shedding shards of ice onto the carpet. Opened the door, and the heat hit her like a soft, welcoming pillow. Light flared as she struck a match and lit the candles on the kitchen table, and she shed her coat and sat down. Pulling her boots off with one hand, she pressed her phone to her ear with the other.

'Fire away, Maisie, I need some good news…'

She heard Maisie's chuckle at the other end of the line. 'Some of the local practices have got together with the healthcare trust to organise a group of volunteers with four-wheel-drive vehicles. The idea is that they'll help doctors and district nurses who are having difficulty getting through to patients. You've got your very own escort for tomorrow.'

Neve swallowed hard. This sounded too good to be true, and if the general trend for today was anything to go by, that meant it was. 'Who? Is he local?'

'Lives in Leminster. He's from Canada, so I suppose he must know a bit about snow.'

'Sounds promising.'

'It is. Joe's a nice guy. Outdoorsy type. Moved here

just before Christmas last year. He was on crutches then, but that was only for a couple of months. He built a front porch for Edie Wilcox last summer and put in grab rails so she could get in and out of the house…'

'Wait… Who's Edie Wilcox?' Maisie had lived in this area all her life and seemed to know the life histories of everyone within a thirty-mile radius.

'She lives in Leminster. Married old Stan Wilcox and they argued for thirty-seven years non-stop until he dropped down dead from a heart attack. She was devastated and didn't go out of the house for a couple of years…'

'She doesn't go out?'

'Oh, that was twenty years ago. She goes out all the time now. Likes to terrorise the tourists in the summer. Edie's a tough old bird and proud with it. She won't let the social services past the front door, but she must have taken a liking to Joe because she let him do a few alterations to her cottage to make it a bit easier for her to get around.'

Neve's head was beginning to swim. Maisie had been invaluable in helping her to settle in and be accepted by the community, but there was always the danger of going into information overload.

'So his name's Joe? The guy with the four-by-four?'

'That's right. Joe Lamont. He was going to call round to see you this evening, just to make contact, but I expect he's missed you if you've only just got home. Did he leave a note?'

'I don't think so. Hold on, I'll go and see.' Neve scooted down the hall to the front door, treading on a piece of ice and feeling it melt through her thick woollen socks. 'No, nothing here.' Shivering, she hurried back to the warmth of the kitchen.

'I'll call him, then, and let him know you'll be in contact.'

'That's okay, I'll call him now…' Neve found a pen and

scribbled the number that Maisie recited onto the back of her hand.

'You're all right out there, are you? You know you can always stay with us.'

'I'm fine. Thanks, Maisie, but I've got all I need.' She had food, heat and plenty of candles. The farmhouse kitchen extended the full width of the back of the house, and was big enough to easily accommodate a table and chairs next to the cooking area, and a sofa bed at the far end by the old stone hearth. Right now, the sofa bed was the only thing she needed.

'Okay. I'll give you a call in the morning. Stay warm.'

A cup of tea, and then she'd call this guy and get some sleep. Neve filled the kettle and set it to boil on the stove.

The front door rattled, as if something heavy had struck it. Neve wondered if she should go and see what it was and decided against it. If that was the porch collapsing under the weight of snow on the roof, then tomorrow morning would be soon enough to find out.

Two more thumps and the muffled sound of a voice. Someone was outside. Neve picked up a candle and ventured into the hall.

Movement, and a flare of light ahead of her made her jump. Stupid, it was just the candle, reflected in the hall mirror. Perhaps it was the flickering light that made her look like something out of a horror movie, a chalk-white face with dark circles under the eyes. Neve grimaced at herself in the glass, swiping her free hand through her unruly blonde curls in an effort to make herself look vaguely presentable.

'Who's there?'

'Joe Lamont. I'm looking for Dr Harrison.'

'What…?' Neve bit her tongue. There wasn't much point in asking what he was doing out on a night like this if she was going to leave him standing on the doorstep. She pulled the door open, and a gust of freezing air blew the candle out, leaving her staring at a large, black shadow.

'Come in. I was about to phone you.'

'Thanks…' The figure kicked his heavy boots against the doorstep, and stepped inside, pushing the door closed behind him. 'Your doorbell isn't working.'

'No, the power's off. Wait there a moment. I'll just open the kitchen door to give us some light…' Suddenly, a torch beam almost blinded her, and a gloved hand found hers.

'Here. Take this.'

For a moment all Neve could register was his smell. Warm and clean, the kind of scent produced by the chemistry of soap and skin, rather than anything you got from a bottle. Then he put the torch into her hand, stepping back almost immediately, as if to give her some space.

'Thanks.' She had a strong temptation to shine the light in the direction of Joe's outline, but Neve resisted it and turned, leading the way through the hallway. 'Come through.'

She shut the kitchen door behind them, watching while Joe pulled his gloves off and unzipped his heavy jacket. He was tall, with what looked like broad shoulders, but that might just be the bulk of his clothing. In the torchlight, his cheekbones looked as sharp as knives.

'Are you okay out here on your own?'

His voice was deep, with the trace of a Canadian accent along with a little of the cadence of the Yorkshire village he'd made his home. The kind of voice you'd want to hear if you were in trouble. Neve almost began to wish she was.

'I'm fine, thanks. I have heat and light.' She switched off the torch, and in the candlelight his features seemed to soften.

He looked around. 'And food?'

'Yes.' Enough to keep her going for another day. 'I'm making tea—would you like a cup?'

His gaze flicked quickly around the room, as if he was still unconvinced about something, then he nodded. 'Thanks. That would be nice.'

'Sit down.' She waved him towards the table. 'And why don't you take your coat off? You'll melt in here.'

He slung his coat over the back of a chair and sat, running one hand absently across the scarred oak tabletop, his fingers seeming to explore the grain. 'You get hot water from the stove?'

'Yes. The power goes out from time to time here, so I had an oil-fired stove put in.' It appeared the questioning wasn't over quite yet. That was okay, he could ask. Neve had made sure that she could deal with pretty much anything the world chose to throw at her, and she had the answers.

The touch of humour that twitched at the sides of his mouth suited him. 'I guess I'll just stop with the neighbourly concern, shall I?'

'It's appreciated. But not needed at the moment.' She hid her smile behind the open door of the larder, reaching for the biscuit barrel and laying it on the table next to the teapot. 'Help yourself.'

He took the mug of tea that she slid across the table towards him with a nod of acknowledgement. He seemed... tense wasn't the word. He seemed watchful, taking in everything around him, as if he needed to keep an eye on the world to keep it spinning. Neve began to wish that she'd found the time to fold the sofa bed back up this morning. Hopefully, any stray underwear would go unnoticed in the candlelight.

'You're not from around here?' His attention was fixed on Neve now and, before she could stop it, her hand flew to her hair to smooth it back. 'The South somewhere?'

'London.'

He nodded. 'I must be improving. When I first came here, all I could hear was that everyone had British accents.'

'And you're from Canada…?'

His smile had the same sense of discipline about it as all his other movements did. Graceful, economical, and with a sense of purpose about it. And gorgeous.

'Right in one. Most people reckon I'm from America.'

'Actually, Maisie told me. I imagine you've got a lot more experience of driving in these conditions than me.' Best get back to business. That smile, the relaxed, watchful curve of his body was distracting her.

'A bit. It's a little different at home…'

'Snow's snow, isn't it?'

'My Inupiak granny wouldn't agree with you there. She lived on the ice when she was a child, and could write a book about different kinds of snow.'

That explained his striking looks. Raven-dark hair that grazed the collar of his thick sweater. Dark eyes and proud cheekbones. 'So how did you end up in Yorkshire?'

'My other grandmother came from around here. Her family went to Canada when she was a child, but she used to tell me stories about England. I decided to pay a visit and ended up staying.' He looked at his tea, as if taking a second sip was yet another thing that required a thought-through decision. 'It's a good base to travel to Europe from.'

Neve would have thought that London would be better. But Joe didn't seem the type to spend much time worrying about what other people thought. 'You travel a lot?'

He shrugged. 'A bit. I've seen most of Europe. Africa, Asia.' He made a small, dismissive movement of his hand, as if this all meant nothing. 'How long have you been here?'

'Eighteen months.'

'Love at first sight?'

'Eh?' Suddenly she was falling into the depths of his dark eyes. Not quite love at first sight, but there was definitely something about him…

'You fell in love with this place. Like me.'

Nothing like that. Yorkshire had been somewhere to run to, and the most lovely thing about this particular location was that it was remote. 'I'm growing to love it. Maisie's been very good to me.'

He nodded. 'She's a force to be reckoned with, isn't she? When she called me, asking for help, there was no saying no…'

'But I thought… Aren't you a volunteer?'

'Seems I am now.'

Neve's heart sank. 'So Maisie talked you into this. Listen, if you don't want—'

'It's okay. I was getting a little cabin crazy doing nothing at home, and I was looking for a way to help. Maisie just saved me some trouble.' His dark gaze sought hers. 'I have winter tyres fitted on my four-by-four, and they'll cope with just about anything. And snow chains, in case we run into any trouble. You'll be quite safe.'

'I don't doubt it.' He didn't need to reassure her. Maisie had vouched for him, and in any case there was something about Joe. If you were in the habit of trusting people on the basis of ten minutes' conversation then he'd be the one to pick.

'Maisie said you were covering the north side of the practice's catchment area.' He reached over and slid a map out of his jacket pocket, spreading it on the table. 'Here…' His finger described a loop.

'Yes, that's right. We've split the practice up into three, and each one of us is covering one section. We're holding temporary surgeries in church halls and so on for people who find it difficult to get to the main surgery, and taking on all the visits for our own area. Cuts down on the travelling.'

'I imagine you're still pretty busy, though.'

'Yeah. With only two weeks to go before Christmas…' She shrugged. 'Everyone seems to rush for the shops and the doctor's surgery around now.'

He nodded, surveying the map thoughtfully. 'You've drawn the short straw, this is some of the most difficult terrain in the area. Couldn't you have asked to swap with a doctor with more local experience?'

Neve felt her spine stiffen. One of the reasons she'd come here was to escape being told what she could, and couldn't, do.

'We each took the area closest to where we live. I can handle it.'

'I dare say you can.' He flashed her a disarming smile. 'What time do you want me tomorrow?'

Six o'clock, with a cup of fresh brewed coffee and a gently warmed croissant. The fantasy was inappropriate on almost every level she could think of, and Neve let it slide.

'If nothing else urgent comes up, I'll be starting in Leminster at nine tomorrow. I can drive over and meet you there…'

He shook his head. 'I'll pick you up at eight-thirty.' He re-folded the map and stood up. 'I'd better get going now. I'm on my way to the supermarket in town…'

'At this time of night?'

'I promised to pick some things up for someone. Can I get you anything?' He gestured towards the large, well-scraped jar sitting on the kitchen worktop. 'Some more peanut butter?'

He didn't give up, did he? But she *was* going to have to

stop off at the shops tomorrow if she didn't ask for more supplies now. 'Um…perhaps one or two things. If it's no trouble.'

'No trouble. Give me a list…'

CHAPTER TWO

A BOWL OF steaming porridge, a banana that had seen better days, coffee, toast and the last of the peanut butter would be enough to keep her going for the morning. By twenty past eight, Neve had tidied up and folded the sofa bed, and her deliberations about whether it was entirely wise to tidy her duvet away upstairs in the freezing bedroom were interrupted by the sound of a car outside in the lane. She dumped the duvet back onto the sofa and ventured into the hall, peering outside.

The trees were laden with snow after a fresh fall during the night. Clear blue skies, and sparkling white fields. The landscape had a kind of rugged beauty about it, an implicit challenge to either respect its rules or fall foul of them.

And talking about rugged beauty…

Joe had just got out of the driver's seat of a black SUV. The high chassis and large wheels looked more than capable of tackling the rough terrain they were going to face today. He looked pretty capable, too. Tall and broad, standing for a moment to assess the sky and the road that twisted away into the distance, then shouldering a large canvas bag and turning towards her house. The gate was packed round with ice and snow and refused to budge, and he swung effortlessly over the low front wall.

It looked a bit eager, but she opened the front door anyway, not waiting for him to knock. 'Hi. You made it...'

He shrugged, as if making it here hadn't been in question. Kicked off his boots and strode into the kitchen, dumping the bag at her feet.

'Hope this is what you wanted...'

Neve bent to look inside the bag. Everything on her list and more. A hand of bananas, a bag of apples and a punnet of strawberries. She looked up at him silently.

'I saw that your bowl was nearly empty.' He gestured towards the one wizened apple in the fruit bowl.

The idea that Joe had been silently noting and assessing everything wasn't particularly comfortable. 'Thanks. That was thoughtful of you.'

'You're welcome.' He fished in his pocket and brought out a note and some change, putting it down on the table.

'Is that right? Surely you spent more than that?'

He shrugged. 'I shopped around. And someone gave me the strawberries yesterday.'

Neve gave him a long, questioning look and then gave up. If Joe wanted to operate on a need-to-know basis, then so be it. She hurried to stow the non-perishables in the larder and then opened the back door, pulling a heavy-duty plastic box inside and putting it on the table.

He was quietly watching her every move, and Neve felt her brow crease with anxiety. That old feeling of having something to prove to someone. She thought she'd left that behind her when she'd turned onto the M1 motorway from London, and headed north.

'Let me...' She was struggling with the clips on the box, and before she could protest he'd spun the box towards him and knocked a lump of ice out from under the lid, wresting it open.

Inside, there was half a pint of milk and a carton of juice, both frozen into solid lumps. One of his eyebrows arched, and Neve felt her hackles rise in response to the unspoken question.

'What…?' She should probably just leave it. Neve tipped the remainder of the shopping into the box and clapped the lid back on, fastening it securely.

'Nothing… If I'd realised you were so short of supplies, I could have brought a few more things in for you.'

'I'm fine. I told you that last night.' She heard herself snap at him and reminded herself that Joe was a volunteer, doing this out of the goodness of his heart, and that she ought to make an effort to get along with him. 'Are we going to get going, then?'

'As soon as you tell me where.' A hint of emotion tugged at the corner of his perfect mouth.

Neve sat down at the kitchen table. Maybe she was overreacting. It wasn't Joe's fault that the quiver in the pit of her stomach whenever she saw him reminded her of all the promises she'd made to herself about never letting a man walk all over her again.

'This is my list. We're due in Leminster first and then whichever order is easiest in terms of the driving.'

'Right.' He pulled the map from his pocket, spreading it on the table, one finger tracing the pattern of the other addresses on the list. 'So if we drive north from Leminster…' He swept his finger across the map in a rough circle, indicating forty miles of driving through blocked roads and over sheets of ice.

'That would be ideal. Can we make it?'

'Let me worry about that.' He picked up his gloves from the kitchen table and folded the map, his frame suddenly taut and eager. A glimmer in his eyes seemed to flash out a warning to the world that obstacles weren't a problem, and only existed to be overcome.

She'd find out soon enough if Joe was as good as his word. Neve picked up one of the bags of medical supplies, which lay ready by the door, and Joe got to the second before she could. 'Let's go, then.'

She was silent as Joe drove along the winding, treacherous road into Leminster village. Wary of him maybe?

Joe dismissed the thought. Neve struck him as the kind of woman who wasn't afraid of anything. When her blue eyes had flashed with stubborn resolve, all his senses had tingled painfully back to life, reminding him that once he'd lived for the kind of challenges she faced now. Her scent and the way she moved only added to the temptation. He dismissed those thoughts as well.

Joe had put himself on trial here. When he'd first come to the village he'd deliberately avoided anything that was even remotely connected with his former life, but now there was a need he could fulfil. If he could do this, without getting involved with the medical side of things, that would be a final step towards putting his old life behind him.

He drew up outside the church hall in Leminster. A surgery had been arranged for those who could make it here, and outside the new fallen snow was already churned and flattened by the passing of feet. Inside, the occasion appeared to have turned into an impromptu coffee morning.

From the relaxed smile on her face when Neve walked into the hall, one would never have guessed that she was probably counting faces, wondering whether she was going to be here all day. She walked briskly into the middle of the noisy throng and clapped her hands.

Silence. Joe allowed himself a smile. That was an achievement in itself.

'Who's here for me?' She made it sound like a party, and that she was excited to see that so many people had turned up. Three-quarters of the hands in the room shot up, and she tried again.

'One hand for each patient, please.'

Most of the hands went back down again, leaving six. She gave a dazzling smile in response and received a low rumble of approbation from the assembled company.

She had a nice way about her. In Joe's experience, if you wanted to know about a doctor, you looked first at their patients. And if the faces here were anything to go by, Neve was one of the best. Her style might be a little different from his, a little more long-lost-relative and a little less here-comes-the-cavalry, but that was no bad thing. Joe reminded himself that he was here to drive, nothing more.

'Who's first?' Someone pointed to Fred Hawkins, sitting in the corner of the room, and he reached for his walking stick.

'That's okay, Fred. Finish your tea, it'll be a couple of minutes before I get settled.' She flashed Joe a smile then turned to the church warden, who guided her away into one of the small rooms at the back of the hall.

Although the intention behind holding a surgery here had not been primarily to carry out a fact-finding mission regarding Joe Lamont, it did turn up a lot of information. Fred Hawkins confided that he was a 'useful enough carpenter' while Neve was trying to listen to his chest. Lisa Graham chattered about him incessantly as Neve examined a lump on her young son's leg, and Ann Hawkins, headmistress of the local primary school and the wife of Fred's second cousin, proffered the information that Joe had built an adventure playground for the school a few months back.

'He was quite a talking point for a while…' Ann winced as Neve removed the dressing from her swollen finger to reveal a cut.

'Do you have any loss of sensation? Here?' Neve worked gently along the main nerves.

'No. It's a real addition for us. The kids love it.'

'Right. I'm going to put some adhesive stitches onto the cut and I'll prescribe antibiotics, just to be on the safe side.'

Ann nodded. 'Thanks. He doesn't seem to have anyone. Not that some of the younger women haven't tried. I had to have a word with one of our teaching assistants about staring out of the window all moony-eyed at him when she was supposed to be doing her job.'

Neve hid a grin. It appeared that Joe-itis wasn't just confined to the teaching assistants. The school's head teacher had been infected with the epidemic as well, along with what sounded like half the village.

'So what exactly does he do?' Neve's curiosity about Joe had been growing, and she gave in to the inevitable. 'His job, I mean.'

'I heard he was ex-army.' Ann pursed her lips thoughtfully. 'I don't know if that's true. He doesn't seem to have a job now. Unless of course he's doing something on the internet in the evenings.'

Professional gambler? She imagined that Joe would have the perfect poker face if he put his mind to it. Writer? Internet entrepreneur? Combination of all three?

'There were a few rumours going round, but they were just idle talk.' Ann dismissed any further speculation with a disapproving twitch of her mouth. 'But, then, people will wonder.'

True enough. The secret to keeping a secret was never to let a soul know that you had one. Neve had never told anyone about her marriage, and so the awkward questions about why it had been such a disaster never occurred to anyone.

'Hold still, Ann. This will sting a little bit.'

Ann winced as Neve cleaned and disinfected the wound. 'He wasn't well, of course, when he first came here. You know his grandmother was born in Leminster? Fred remembers her from way back, when he was just a boy. Says she was a pretty little thing.'

Perhaps that was why the village had taken Joe to their hearts. The prodigal son returned. But in Neve's experience, any respect you got from the close-knit communities around here was generally earned and not just doled out on account of who your grandmother was.

'Right, then, Ann.' She handed her the prescription. 'I want you to take these for a week. Can you get to the chemist today?'

'Yes, no problem.' Ann got to her feet. 'I suppose you're back on the road again now. You must be busy.'

'Yes. It's a lot easier with Joe doing the driving, though.'

'Mmm. With the weather like this, you need someone to help you.'

By the time Neve had finished, Joe had been persuaded up a ladder to fix Christmas decorations to the high ceiling beams and had helped move the piano to make room for the Christmas tree. It was something of a relief to retrieve his coat and follow her back outside to the car.

'What's that you've got?' She nodded at the plastic food container in his hand.

'Chocolate cake. I said it was a bit early for me, so there are two large pieces here for later.' He wondered whether she'd greet this latest offer of food with the same prickly indignation she'd shown that morning.

'Oh, nice. I like chocolate cake.' She had a particular flair for confounding his expectations, and Joe found himself smiling.

The first real obstacle of the day presented itself a mile down the road, in the shape of a white minibus. It was blocking the road ahead, almost invisible against the drifting snow, only the bright flash of a logo on its side clearly distinguishable.

Joe slowed and stopped. 'Television crew.'

'How do you know that?'

'I heard they've been filming around Leminster. Community in crisis, that kind of thing.'

Neve was frowning at the vehicle. 'Looks as if the community's dealing with the crisis a bit better than they are.'

'Yeah. Perhaps they can film themselves.'

The sound of a racing engine drifted towards them and the wheels of the minibus spun uselessly. Joe swung out of the car. 'Hey. Hold up. That's not going to get you anywhere…' he called over to the driver and the engine stopped abruptly. One of the doors opened and a woman got out.

Joe knew what was needed, and it didn't take much to persuade the woman to leave things to him. He trudged back to his own vehicle, nodding grimly at Neve and opening the tailgate.

'What are we going to do?' She scrambled out of her seat, almost losing her balance on a patch of ice and grabbing at him to steady herself.

'Maybe you should stay in the car.' Much as he liked her weight on his arm, it wasn't going to get the van on its way.

'What, and comb my hair? Check my make-up?'

Joe straightened up. However much he got snagged on her protective spikes, he still couldn't help but smile at her. Maybe it was the vulnerability behind that tough exterior. Or the bravery that met everything head on. 'If you use the rear-view mirror, don't forget to adjust it back the way you found it.'

A moment of fleeting outrage and then she relaxed. 'Sorry. It's just that I've been managing on my own for a while now…'

'I know.'

She leaned back against the car. 'So what are you going to do?'

'I should be able to dig them out. Might need to give them a tow but I hope not. It'll take time to get the snow chains on the wheels to give me the extra traction.'

'What's that for?' She pointed to the large bag of cat litter that he'd dumped in the snow beside them.

'It'll soak up the water around the wheels and give something for them to grip onto.' Joe reached for the fold-up shovel that he'd stowed in the boot, snapping it open.

'You have a cat?' No detail was too small to escape her interest and Joe couldn't help grinning.

'Why would I have cat litter if I don't have a cat?' He picked up the bag and started to trudge back towards the stricken minibus.

'Let me know if you need a hand,' she called after him.

'Sure. Let me know if you can't find your comb.'

Neve remained where she was, leaning against the side of the SUV. Two men had got out of the minibus and Joe had set one of them to work with the shovel while he spread the cat litter around the wheels. The woman Joe had been talking to had left them to it and was headed in Neve's direction.

'I'm glad you guys turned up.' She was grinning brightly. 'Your friend seems to know what to do. What are you doing out today?'

'I'm a doctor. I have house calls to make.'

'Ah.' The woman nodded enthusiastically. 'And your partner?' She gestured over towards Joe. 'He's a doctor too?'

'He's a volunteer. He's helping with the driving.'

'Nice one. As we're stranded here, perhaps you could give me an interview.' The woman didn't wait for Neve's answer and gestured over to the second man, who was standing by the stricken vehicle, watching Joe. 'Camera, Nick…'

'I don't think we have time. We have to get on…'

'Just for a minute. We won't keep you.'

Neve bit back the temptation to say that the news crew was already keeping them, by dint of their minibus blocking the road. 'I have patients…'

'I promise we'll be finished before you know it. Or you could go over there and pretend to help, if you prefer.'

No, she didn't prefer. The last thing Neve wanted to do was to embarrass herself with Joe by pretending to help him for the cameras.

'Joe…' She marched over to the minibus, where he was now shovelling ice and snow from under the chassis. 'We'll be going soon, won't we?'

He straightened, taking in the hastily assembled tripod and camera. 'She's asked you for an interview, hasn't she?'

Neve shifted uncomfortably. 'Yes. But I've told them there's no time. We have to be on our way…'

He grinned. Joe was enjoying her discomfiture a little too much. 'I'm afraid it'll be a short while yet. And I don't dig well with an audience. Perhaps you can keep them amused for a few minutes.'

'Thanks a lot.'

He shrugged. 'Thought you wanted to help.'

Not what she'd had in mind. Neve turned on her heel and walked back to the camera.

'Ready?' The woman smiled brightly at her. 'Perhaps if you could take your hat off so we can see your face.'

She was going to have to do this. Neve stood on the spot the reporter indicated and removed her hat, smiling uneasily. The camera swept across the snow-covered hills and then homed in on her.

'How are you coping in these difficult conditions? Are your patients going without the medical help they need?'

An image of Maisie on the phone, reassuring worried callers that the doctor would be able to see them, flashed through Neve's mind. 'No, we're seeing everyone. We're coping very well.'

'But your resources must be strained to breaking point. How long can you go on like this?'

'As long as we need to. We expect snow during the winter here, and we plan for it. It's business as usual, and that's not going to change.' Neve tried to put all the gravitas of her profession behind the statement. Difficult when a blast of icy wind had just slapped the side of her face, almost taking her breath away and making her nose drip.

The sound of the minibus's engine choking into life saved her. Joe was in the driver's seat, gently rolling the vehicle forward and out of the patch of slush that its spinning wheels had produced.

'Sorry. Got to go.' Neve almost skipped over to where the empty cat-litter bag and the shovel lay, picked them up and carried them back to Joe's car. Then she got in, shutting the door firmly. The news crew took one last shot of Joe walking back to the SUV, then there was a scramble to get the camera packed up and they were on their way, Joe following the minibus as it nosed its way along the narrow, snow-filled lane.

As soon as the road widened, he flashed his headlights and a brief, assertive blast of the horn signalled the driver of the minibus to pull over. Joe overtook it, and in a sudden show of bravado he put his foot down, a shower of powdery snow flying up from the wheels as they accelerated away.

'Show-off.'

He chuckled. 'You looked a bit put out by some of those questions.'

He'd noticed. No surprise there, Joe seemed to notice everything. 'Well, really. What did they expect me to do?

Go on TV saying that my patients will be lucky to get a visit this side of next week?'

'I imagine that's what they wanted to hear.'

'Well, tough. I'll make it through to everyone…' It occurred to Neve that Joe had a part in that now. 'I meant *we.*'

He gave her a melting grin. 'Yeah. We'll make it.'

After eleven hours, half of it spent huddled in the passenger seat of his car and the other half seeing her patients, Neve still shone. In Joe's experience, that took some doing. When they drew up outside her house that evening, she heaved a deep sigh of contentment.

'Look…'

He looked. Welcoming light glowed from the porch. 'Your power's back on?'

'Yes.' Her smile made it seem like the end of a perfect day, rather than the first piece of good luck that she hadn't had to work hard for. 'Will you come in for tea?'

The warmth of her rambling farmhouse kitchen. The warmth of her smile. In a past life, which seemed so distant now it was if it had all happened to someone else, Joe wouldn't have hesitated to say yes.

'No. Thanks, but I should get going. I'll see you in the morning. Same time?'

'Tomorrow's Saturday. Aren't you taking the weekend off?'

'Are you?'

She shrugged. 'Not this weekend. I'll be off next weekend.'

'Then I'll see you in the morning. Eight-thirty.'

Her smile made the whole day worthwhile. 'Shall we say nine? I think we both deserve a lie-in.'

'Nine it is.'

'Thanks for all you've done today, Joe. I really appreciate it.'

It had been his pleasure. Having her rely on him, bringing her safely home again had made Joe feel strong again. As if he'd flexed muscles that had been long under-used and had found, almost to his disbelief, that they had taken the strain. But he shouldn't go too far.

He carried her bags up the path for her, setting them down on the doorstep and turning back, before the lure of refreshments got too great. Got into his SUV and waited until she was safely inside the house before he started the engine and drove away. Neve was just the kind of woman who could tempt a man into believing that he could be whatever he wanted to be. And in Joe's experience, the one good thing about having found your breaking point was that you knew for sure that some things were out of reach.

CHAPTER THREE

'HOW ARE WE going with the list?'

The list had been the overarching purpose of their lives for the last three days. How many people were on it and where they lived. It was a challenge and a reason for Neve to spend her days with him. Joe was getting to love the list.

However much he loved it, he didn't get to spend a lot of quality time with it. While she let him get on with his side of things, assessing their route, driving and the odd spell of snow clearing, the list was Neve's responsibility, and she seemed to function best when it was under her control.

'Not bad. Just four more. We need to go up to Holcombe Crag, and there are three more between there and Leminster.'

'Where first?' Joe had no inclination to involve himself in the decisions about who needed her most urgently, and was always careful to let Neve set their priorities.

'What do you think? I guess it would be better to go up to Holcombe Crag while it's still light.' She reached for the bag of toffees on the dashboard, offering him one, and when he shook his head she unwrapped one for herself.

'Probably, but don't worry about that. If the others need to be seen first...'

'No, they're all routine visits. They could wait until

tomorrow morning if we don't get time today, but Nancy Olsen's got a young baby so I'd like to see her this afternoon.'

Joe nodded, and started the car. 'Holcombe Crag it is, then.'

Neve had been watching the clouds draw across the sky as they approached the crag. 'Are we going to make this? It looks as if the weather's closing in.'

'We'll make it. There's plenty of time to get up there and back before it gets dark— Is that your phone, or mine?'

'Mine, I think.' Neve unzipped her jacket and pulled her phone from the inside pocket, studying the small screen. 'It's a text from Maisie.'

'Another house call?'

Neve shook her head and read from the screen. *"'Local radio news. Car carrying father and young son found abandoned in your area this morning. Search under way. Keep your eyes open."'*

Neve texted a short acknowledgement back to Maisie and put her phone back into her pocket. 'Anyone walking in this weather is going to be freezing.'

Joe nodded, his brow creased. 'Hopefully they've been able to find some shelter. Shame they didn't stay with the car.'

'I hope they find them soon.'

'Yeah. When we get to Holcombe Crag I'll take a look around. Might get lucky.'

He turned off and took the track that climbed towards Holcombe Crag. At the best of times it was a steep hill to climb, but now the ice and snow seemed an impossible barrier. But Joe took it calmly and steadily, confident of what the vehicle could do and not asking the impossible from it. He drew up outside the single-storey, stone-built house, which clung to the slope three-quarters of the way up the crag.

'If I walk up to the top, I'll get a much better view.' He'd extracted a pair of field glasses from the boot of his car, which seemed increasingly to Neve like an Aladdin's cave of useful items. 'How long will you be?'

'I think Nancy would appreciate some a little extra time.' Neve looked at her watch. 'Shall we meet back here in half an hour?'

He nodded, dropping his car keys into her hand. Joe always carried her bags from the car, and this sudden break with what had become a small, comfortable ritual between them unsettled her. He must be worried.

She watched as he strode away from her. Strong, steadfast. However much she tried not to depend on him, however misguided it felt to allow any man to shape her fate, he was still becoming an indispensable support to her in this hostile landscape. She dismissed the thought and turned towards the house.

When Nancy opened the door, beckoning her inside, the smell of baking bread assailed her, and Neve's mouth began to water. 'Thanks for coming, Doctor. I'm so sorry to bring you all this way, but I'm worried about Daniel...'

Neve laid a reassuring hand on her arm. 'I'd rather you called if you have any concerns at all. Let's take a look at him.'

Neve was taking her time with each patient, aware that asking someone to pop back to the surgery if things got any worse wasn't a viable option for most people at the moment. But after a careful examination, she found baby Daniel was suffering from no more than a slight cold. Neve reassured Nancy and allowed herself to be tempted into the kitchen for fresh-baked bread and strawberry jam.

'Will you hold him while I put the kettle on?' Nancy smiled down at her son, and he stretched his arms up towards her face, mimicking her expression.

'I'll make the tea.' The bond between them was so precious, too beautiful to break, even for a moment. Neve couldn't help feeling a little stab of envy.

'That's okay.' Daniel gurgled with joy as Nancy planted a kiss on his forehead, before delivering him into Neve's arms. 'See you later, my sunshine...'

Daniel's tiny fingers curled around hers when she tickled his palm and he looked up at her solemnly. Neve no longer had to steel herself to be around babies. The pain of her own loss had slowly given way to gnawing regret for what might have been, and when she smiled at Daniel and he rewarded her with one of his own, everything was suddenly right with the world.

'Can you see Joe?'

Nancy leaned across the sink to get a better view out of the window. 'No. He was at the top a few minutes ago, but he must be on his way back here now.' Nancy turned, seeming to need the reassurance of checking once again that her own child was safe. 'I can't stop thinking about them out there. I hope someone finds them soon.'

'Have you heard any search helicopters?'

'Yes, I heard one go over about half an hour before you got here. I called Daryl when I heard about it on the radio and asked him to keep his eyes open.'

Word of mouth. Passed from wife to husband, friend to friend. Everyone in the area would be on the alert. 'They'll find them.'

Nancy grimaced. 'I hope so. It's snowing again and it'll be dark soon.'

Neve's phone rang, and she fished it out of her pocket one handed. 'Yes?'

'I see them. The man's on his feet, and walking. I'm on my way to them now.' Joe was breathing heavily, as if he was running.

'Where are you? I'll come out and meet you…'

'No… Neve, listen. I need you to stay there…'

It wasn't a matter of what Joe needed. 'I'm a doctor. I can help these people…'

'Which is why you need to organise things there. You can't get to them before I do, and our first priority is to get them into the warmth. I'll bring them to you…'

He was right. Neve didn't like it very much, but this wasn't the time to be squabbling over who did what. 'Okay. We'll get things ready to receive them here. Call me when you reach them and let me know what condition they're in.'

A grunt of assent came down the line and then it cut off. Joe must be putting all his energy into getting to the man and his son.

'What can I do?' Nancy took little Daniel from Neve's arms and put him into his baby bouncer.

'We need somewhere warm to bring them.'

'Okay, the sitting room's best. I've got a fire going in there.'

'That's great. Have you got some spare blankets or a duvet we can use?'

'Yes, of course. What about a hot bath?'

'No, not until we see what condition they're in.' If the man and his son had been out for any length of time in these conditions, the boy could well be hypothermic, his smaller body less able to resist the freezing conditions than an adult's. Warming him too quickly could cause shock or heart problems.

The smile on Nancy's face told Neve that she knew nothing about that, just that the man and his son had been found. Neve hoped that her bright optimism turned out to be justified, and set about helping to warm blankets and fill hot-water bottles.

Just as the wait for Joe's call was becoming intolerable, her phone rang again.

'Joe…'

'I'm with them. The boy's shivering and drowsy but conscious. The man's able to walk.'

Joe wasn't wasting any words, but that was all she needed to know. If the boy was still shivering, then his small body hadn't given up its fight to stay warm yet. 'Okay, that's good. Can you get back here with them?'

'That's the plan…'

'Right. I want you to carry the boy. Be sure to do it carefully, Joe. You must avoid bumping him around any more than absolutely necessary. That's important.' Hopefully the boy wasn't cold enough yet to make him susceptible to internal injuries, but without seeing him Neve couldn't be sure.

'Gotcha. I understand that precaution. I want you to do something for me.'

'Yes…' Anything.

'We're about a mile from you, in a westerly direction. I want you to turn my car and put the headlights on, full beam. Stay on the line, I can hear you through the earpiece. Do it now.'

'Okay, on my way.' Why did he want her to do that? It didn't matter. Neve slung on her coat, grabbed the car keys and signalled to Nancy that she'd be five minutes.

She heaved a sigh of relief when the car started first time. Carefully she manoeuvred it until it was at right angles to the house, hoping that this was in approximately the right direction.

'Joe… Joe…?'

'I see you. Move about ten degrees to your right…'

She rolled the car forward and then back again, turning

in the direction he'd told her, frantic tears forming in her eyes. She could see the reasoning behind this now. The storm that had been threatening was now right overhead, the light was beginning to fail and it was snowing heavily. Neve couldn't see Joe, and it followed that he probably couldn't see the house. The lights were a beacon for him.

'How's that?'

'Good…' His breath was coming fast now, and he must already be walking. Every step brought him nearer. 'One more thing…'

'Yes, Joe. I hear you.' Neve wanted to stretch out and pull him back to her. If willpower alone could have done it, then he was already home and dry.

'If we don't make it back, I want you to stay where you are. You can't find us in these conditions. All that will happen is you'll get lost as well. Have you called the emergency services?'

'Yes, I got on to Maisie. She's liaising with them.'

'Great. Sit tight and wait for them… We're on our way, a mile out in the direction of the beam of the headlights. Have you got all that?'

She couldn't answer. Couldn't tell him that she'd just leave him out there if he didn't return.

'Have you got that, Neve? Say it…'

'Got it, Joe.' It wasn't going to happen. It was only a mile. He could walk that, even in these conditions.

'Good.' Another pause, as Joe caught his breath. 'See you soon.'

She wanted to tell him to come back to her, but she couldn't find a way to say it. 'Yeah. Very soon.' She almost choked on the words. And then determination took over. 'Stay on the line, Joe. I'm going to keep talking…'

'Yeah… Good girl…'

'Girl?' She grinned desperately at her phone. 'I'll give

you *girl*, Joe Lamont. You get back here now, and I'll show you...' Just how much of a woman she was.

'Yes, ma'am...'

'Shut up and walk...'

Nancy's husband Daryl had been summoned from his workshop, which lay thirty feet to the rear of the house, but there was nothing that he could do, other than wait. Neve sent him inside with Nancy, asking them to stay by the phone and keep Maisie updated. She stayed in the car, talking to Joe, straining her eyes into the increasing gloom for any sign of him.

He was beginning to weaken. She could hear it in the few words that he managed to spare for her. His voice was shaking from the cold, and from the effort of walking through the snow. Neve looked at her watch. He must be close by now. Maybe if she went to the edge of the beam of the car headlamps, she'd see him.

Joe had told her to stay here. Ordered her to stay here, actually. And she'd obeyed him. When had that started to happen? The inevitable consequences of that particular slippery slope were suddenly forgotten. She caught her breath, staring into the swirling snow, and slowly the shapes of two men became visible. Joe's jacket was wrapped around the bundle in his arms, which must be the child. A man stumbled alongside him, relying on him for both support and direction.

'I see you, Joe...'

He didn't reply. Just kept walking. Neve wrenched the car door open, stumbling towards Joe, vaguely aware that Daryl had appeared from the house and was running towards the small group. They both reached them at the same time and Daryl took the man's arm, winding it around his shoulders and supporting him towards the house.

She took Joe's arm, and he seemed to straighten, re-

lieved of the burden of the man he'd been supporting.
Something stopped Neve from taking the bundle from
his arms. He'd carried the boy for a long, painful mile, and
he deserved to be the one to bring him inside.

When Nancy ushered them into the hallway, Joe gave
up his precious cargo, delivering the boy into Neve's arms.
'The boy…Charlie. Four years old…F-father…Michael.'

Neve felt Charlie moving fitfully against her. Quickly
she looked around, assessing the situation as best she
could. Joe's waterproof trousers and heavy boots had kept
his legs dry, but his sweater was wringing wet and he was
shivering, from cold and exhaustion. Michael had a heavy
coat on and seemed dry, but looked near to collapse.

'Daryl, take Michael through to the sitting room. Nancy,
will you help Joe, please? Get those wet clothes off him.'
Neve followed Daryl through, laying Charlie down on the
blankets that were warming by the fire.

Carefully she stripped the boy of his coat and welling-
tons. By some miracle, Charlie was dry. It was a hard-won
miracle, though. His father must have carried him for miles
to keep his legs dry in the snow, and Joe had wrapped his
own coat around him to protect him from the snowstorm.

Daryl was helping Michael off with his coat and into
a chair by the fireside. 'Daryl, will you check that none
of Michael's clothes are wet, please? I'll come and look at
him in a minute.'

'No… See to Charlie. Please…' Michael's agonised
voice.

'That's what I'm doing, Michael. Stay where you are
and rest now.'

Neve had already taken the things she'd need from
her medical bag and they lay ready for her. Quickly she
checked Charlie's pulse and reactions. Good. Better than
she'd hoped. The low-temperature thermometer read 32
degrees. Much better than she'd dared hope.

All the same, she followed the guidelines for a more severe case. Wrapping the baby hot-water bottles that Nancy had prepared, she placed them under his arms and at his groin. Then she wrapped Charlie's body in the duvet, leaving his arms and legs free.

A tear squeezed from beneath Charlie's closed eyelids, and Neve bent over him to hold him still and give him some comfort. 'Okay, Charlie. You're all right. Lie still for me, sweetheart.'

'Dad…' The little boy let out a whimper, which stretched into a moan.

'Charlie…' Michael's voice came from behind her.

'Your dad's here, you can see him in a minute.' Charlie's eyes opened. Took their time focussing on her, but surely and steadily found her smile. 'Hello, there, sweetie.'

'Charlie…do what the doctor tells you, darling. Daddy's here…' Michael's voice broke, as if he was crying.

'He's doing well, Michael. You did a good job, keeping him dry. He has mild hypothermia, but I'm warming him now and he should be fine.' Neve allowed herself to hope that the worst was over.

CHAPTER FOUR

SHE HAD EXAMINED Charlie thoroughly. No sign of frostbite and his core temperature was beginning to rise a little. Michael had allowed her to check his pulse and reactions quickly, before sending her back to Charlie's side.

Nancy appeared in the doorway, alone.

'Is Joe all right?' Neve had suppressed the urge to go to him, knowing that Charlie and Michael were her first priorities.

'Yes. I sorted out a sweater of Daryl's and he shooed me out of the bedroom.' Nancy grinned at Neve. 'Guess he's shy.'

Neve suppressed a smile, trying hard not to think about what Joe had to be shy about. 'Go and knock on the door. Make sure he's all right and tell him to come in here, by the fire.'

'Right. Daryl, will you go and check on the soup I've got on the stove?' Nancy disappeared, and Daryl got up from his perch on the arm of the sofa, leaving Neve alone with Michael and Charlie.

'Michael, I'm going to take your boots off and have a look at your toes.' She bent down at his feet.

'Please…' Michael shifted his feet away from her. 'You should be with Charlie.'

'Charlie's right here, Michael. I've already examined him very carefully.'

'No.' Michael's jaw set stubbornly. 'You don't have my permission. Now, go to Charlie.'

Legally speaking, there wasn't much Neve could do. Michael might be under stress, but he was certainly competent to make this decision. In his place, she would have done the same herself.

'Michael, I assure you that I've done everything I can for Charlie—'

'I know the law. I can and will prosecute you for assault if you lay one finger on me.' Michael's eyes were blazing. And Neve knew that all the medical knowledge in the world wasn't going to help him if he wouldn't allow her to touch him.

Joe towelled himself dry and pulled on the T-shirt and sweater that Nancy had left out for him on the bed. He wasn't shivering so badly now, but he knew that the cold ache in his bones would take a while to subside.

He sat down on the bed, resisting the temptation to wrap himself in as many blankets as he could find, curl up and sleep. Maybe there was something he could do to help Neve.

She'd given him no quarter when he had been out in the snow, straining to see the lights from the car. She hadn't cajoled him on or spoken soft words of encouragement, she'd bullied him forward, her voice stronger and more compelling than the storm. He couldn't help smiling to himself when he wondered whether she'd consider carrying out some of those threats she'd made.

There was a knock on the door and Nancy's voice sounded. 'Neve wants to know whether you're okay in there. I'm making a hot drink.'

The rejuvenating feeling that Neve hadn't forgotten about him drove Joe to his feet. 'Thanks, Nancy. Just coming.'

As he approached the sitting room he heard Michael's voice, raised in panicky desperation, and Neve's quieter tones.

'I know the law. I can and will prosecute you for assault if you lay one finger on me.' Michael was pointing to Charlie, insisting that Neve return to his son. Joe's respect for the man grew.

'Neve, why don't you go to Charlie and I'll help Michael with his boots?'

She turned at the sound of Joe's voice, her gaze searching his face. He knew what she was looking for. Some sign that he was up to the job he'd just appropriated for himself. Beckoning him over, she spoke quietly to him.

'You must be very careful. If he has frostbite you can damage his toes very easily. Don't rub his feet to warm them...'

Joe nodded. 'I've been trained in dealing with cold-weather injuries. I've seen frostbite before.' And somehow he just couldn't let go, even though he knew he should. The exhilaration when he knew he'd found Michael and Charlie, the rush of achievement when he'd carried Charlie into the house were still too recent to let him back away now.

She thought for a moment then made her decision. 'Okay. But talk to me, Joe. Tell me everything you see, and let me make the decisions on treatment.'

'Understood. You're the boss.'

He summoned up a relaxed smile and moved over towards Michael. 'Guess you drew the short straw, mate. Let *me* help you.'

Michael nodded, leaning towards him. 'I'm sorry...'

'You don't need to apologise.' Joe almost envied Michael. The kind of love that had driven him on through miles of freezing terrain, and then to reject Neve's offer of help so she could tend to Charlie, was something special. Something that Joe had once wanted for himself, but had given up on.

Michael nodded. 'Dr Harrison…'

'Neve.' She turned to face Michael. 'My name's Neve.'

Michael nodded. 'Neve…I'm sorry, I shouldn't have shouted at you…'

'Don't be. Charlie's a lucky kid to have a father who cares so much about him.'

The tenderness in her eyes would have made a stone weep. Suddenly there didn't seem as if there was enough air in the room for the four of them, and Joe instinctively held his breath.

'We're both lucky that you and Joe were there when we needed you.' Michael spoke quietly.

She gave Michael a smile.

Joe thought the responsibilities that she shouldered for her patients, the ones that Michael shouldered as a parent, were the kind of privilege that *he* had shown himself to be unworthy of. But maybe, just for this afternoon, he could help them both.

'Let's get your boots off now, eh?' Michael didn't argue and Joe reached for the laces, untying them and easing his boots open as far as they would go before he slipped them off. Then his socks. Neve nodded in approval when he asked her to double-check Michael's toes, and Joe tucked a warm blanket around his feet, turning his attention to Michael's hands.

'The last two fingers on his left hand are swollen and red. They feel cold and hard to the touch. No blisters.' He knew this was frostbite, but still he kept his word, relaying everything he saw to Neve without any diagnosis.

'Okay.' Neve turned to look, giving him a quick nod. 'I don't want to attempt rewarming unless we know that we can complete it. I'll give Maisie a call, see what's happening with Search and Rescue.'

'I should have stayed with the car.' Michael was shaking his head, his eyes still fixed on Charlie, as Neve pulled her phone out of her pocket.

'Hindsight's always twenty-twenty.' Joe didn't have the heart to tell Michael that he was right.

'This is all my fault…'

'Hey. Enough of that. You carried Charlie for miles to keep him dry. Never underestimate how important that was.'

'If it wasn't for me, he wouldn't have been in that situation in the first place.'

'I heard that your car ran off the road.' Neve had finished her call and put her phone down on the floor beside Charlie's makeshift bed.

'Yes, we skidded on a patch of ice and ended up in the ditch.' Michael shook his head. 'The battery on my mobile was flat, we've got no power at home, and we stayed in the car for a while. No one came by and I thought that I could walk to the next village, but I got lost. So stupid…'

'You were pretty shaken up by the accident?' Her question seemed casual, but Joe was beginning to divine where she was headed with this.

'Yeah. I couldn't think straight…' Michael began to realise where this was going too. 'It's no excuse.'

'You probably couldn't think straight because you were in mild shock. A car accident will do that.' Joe added his own voice to reinforce Neve's point. 'You acted on instinct, and that instinct was all about getting Charlie to safety.'

Michael fell silent. If he couldn't bring himself to agree, at least he was thinking about it. Joe caught Neve's eye and she shot him a smile.

'What did Maisie say?'

'Search and Rescue are sending a couple of vehicles.

One's fitted out as an ambulance and they'll be able to take Michael and Charlie straight to the hospital.' She shrugged. 'Apparently the helicopter's a no-go.'

'Yeah, they can't land in this visibility.'

She gave him a long look. Joe's mask had slipped again, this time unintentionally.

'That's good to know.' Her tone left him in no doubt that there would be questions later. 'So we'll commence rewarming Michael's fingers. We'll need a bowl of warm water...'

'Thirty-seven to thirty-nine degrees centigrade. For thirty minutes.' He was teasing her now, showing off. Or maybe just trying to reassure her that he knew what he was doing and that she'd been right to trust him. 'Aspirin?'

'Yes, there's a packet in my bag.' She looked up at him, her wry grin taunting Joe. 'I'm sure you haven't forgotten the list of contra-indications...'

By the time the rescue team arrived, Charlie was awake and alert, seemingly none the worse for his experience. Michael had seemed to gain in strength as soon as he'd seen that his son was doing well, and under Neve's watchful eye both of them had managed to drink some soup.

'They'll be all right?' Nancy blinked back the tears when she planted a kiss on Charlie's forehead, before the little boy was bundled up in blankets, ready for his trip to the hospital.

'I'll call in the morning and make sure. They're safe now.' Neve took her hand and squeezed it. So much had happened this afternoon. Everyone had played their part in keeping little Charlie safe.

'I guess we should be on our way too...' Joe was reaching for his coat. 'We can't thank you enough, Nancy.'

Nancy shrugged. 'The word "privilege" springs to mind.'

She'd summed it up completely. Neve had seen her share

of people fight for life in a hospital setting, but somehow this was so much more raw, so immediate. Now that it was over, Neve wanted to retreat into a corner and weep at the thought of the sum of human endeavour that had wrought today's miracle.

Strike that. She wanted to cling to Joe and weep. Then she had a couple of questions for him.

She gave Nancy a brief hug, pulling away before the lump in her throat strangled her. 'Thanks for everything. I'll call you in the morning.'

The front door opened and Daryl burst in, bringing a blast of cold air with him. 'I don't think you two are going anywhere tonight.' He dropped Joe's car keys into his hand. 'I got the worst of the snow off the car and went to start the engine to clear the windows. The battery's flat.'

Neve's hand flew to her mouth. That was her fault. In the joy of seeing Joe and Michael emerge from the storm and her haste to get them inside, she had forgotten to switch the car headlights off.

'Joe…I'm so sorry…' He was sure to be angry with her. Who wouldn't be?

He dismissed her crime with a shrug. 'No problem. I've got a set of jump-leads.' He turned to Daryl. 'If you can give me a start, I'll take the car for a run to charge the battery up and come back for Neve.'

'You will not!' Nancy glared at him as if he'd just suggested burning the house down. 'I'll get some dinner and you'll both stay here tonight. Daryl can plug the battery in to charge in the garage.'

'That's too much trouble…' Neve was caught agonisingly between two sets of inconvenience that her mistake was going to cause. She didn't want Joe out there on his own in this weather, but Nancy and Daryl had already done enough.

'Nah.' Daryl grinned at her. 'If you want trouble, try telling Nance that you're not staying.'

Nancy nodded. 'And while I'm making dinner you can go over to Daryl's workshop. He's got a few new designs that he's dying to show off…'

The no-nonsense, make-yourself-at-home hospitality hadn't once suggested that Neve was at fault for the dead battery. It had just been one of those things. Daryl had spent a while in his workshop with Joe, and when Neve had been sent over to fetch them for dinner, they had been deep in conversation over the custom-made furniture that was the product of Daryl's growing small business.

Neve was shown to the spare room, and a bed was made up for Joe in the sitting room. Nancy and Daryl bade them an early goodnight, leaving them sitting together by the fire.

'I suppose I should turn in as well.' Neve wasn't tired, and the events of the day were still jostling for attention in her head, but now that she was alone with Joe she didn't know how to ask the questions that had been bugging her all afternoon.

'Yeah? Not on my account. I'll be staying up a while longer.' He was sunk deep into an armchair, his legs stretched out in front of him.

'Are you okay?'

'Why wouldn't I be?' A question to deflect a question.

'I noticed you were…limping a little.'

'When did you notice that?' The soft words were a challenge. Only go here if you dare.

'When I was walking behind you, on the way back from Daryl's workshop. You were favouring your right leg.' She met his gaze and remembered warmth tingled through her senses. That same intimate connection that had seemed to reach out and pull Joe from the cold embrace of the storm. 'I'm a doctor. I notice these things.'

He nodded. 'It's an old injury. I still limp a little when I'm tired. It's nothing.'

'Are you sure? I can take a look…' Here, at the warm fireside, taking a look was unlikely to remain strictly professional. It might not be a good idea. But, then, Neve's reasons for asking weren't strictly professional either, however much she wanted to pretend they were.

'I'm fine. Truly.' The silence in the room enveloped them. Warm, melting, as if they were curled up together beneath a thick blanket.

'Comminuted fracture of the left femur.' He smiled lazily. 'You were looking at my legs.'

'Was I?' More like staring. Neve felt herself redden.

'I have a titanium intramedullary nail.' He laid his hand on his left leg, splaying his fingers as if to shield it. 'Eighteen months ago. Pretty much a complete recovery.'

She was trying not to think about the force that it took to break the long, sturdy bone that ran from his hip to his knee. 'That…must have hurt.'

'Yeah. At the time. They did a good job of patching me back up, though.'

There was something more. Something floating in the air between them that Neve couldn't quite catch hold of. Maybe she was just tired.

'I should go to bed.' She got unsteadily to her feet. 'I'll see you in the morning.'

'Yeah. I'm going to sit up for a while.'

Was that an invitation? Or just a statement of fact? It was difficult to tell what Joe was thinking at the best of times, and it would be good to go now, before she said something that she was going to regret in the morning.

'Goodnight, then.'

'Neve…'

'Yes…?'

'Thanks for…' He broke off for a moment, staring thoughtfully into the fire. 'I heard every word you said. On the phone.'

Her cheeks were burning now. Exactly what *had* she said? She could hardly remember. 'I'm…I'm sorry, I…'

'Don't be.' He cut her off abruptly. 'At one point I was practically carrying both Michael and Charlie and I didn't think I could go much further. Then you told me to move my sorry arse.'

Neve winced. 'I said that?'

'Yes.' He looked up at her, his gaze threading its way into the pleasure centres of her brain. 'I think your exact words were…'

He broke off as her cheeks burned redder. 'I forget your exact words.'

She remembered them now. And it was definitely time to leave. 'Right. Good. Sleep well.'

He flashed her a grin. 'Goodnight.'

Joe walked into the kitchen, ran water into a glass and took long swallows from it. Perhaps he'd been living the quiet life for too long here. Today had been a taste of his old life—the challenges, the keen exhilaration of overcoming them. Only there had been a difference. Before he'd been fighting for a principle, an abstract notion of saving the world. Today it was Neve that he'd come back to, her face that he'd imagined in front of him in the snow.

He needed to take it down a notch. Things had worked out today, but he couldn't rely on that. Couldn't rely on himself to come through on a regular basis, and in Neve's world that was what you needed to do. That was what he had needed to do, and he'd been found wanting.

Joe returned to the sitting room, laying the quilt from his bed for the night on the floor in front of the fire. Slipped off his jeans and sweater and sat down on the quilt. He'd done this practically every night for a year now, and it calmed him and helped him to sleep.

Closing his eyes, he worked his fingers along his leg, massaging the knotted muscles. Stretching his legs, and then his arms and shoulders. Letting his mind and body relax into the familiar routine. Almost…almost banishing her face from his thoughts.

CHAPTER FIVE

NEVE SAT ON the bed in the spare room, staring at the nightdress that Nancy had left out for her. She could hear Joe moving around quietly in the kitchen. Then silence.

She padded to the door and looked out into the hallway, unable to shake the feeling that there was still unfinished business between her and Joe. The sitting-room door was ajar, a line of light filtering round it. Unthinkingly, with the mistaken instinct of a moth attracted to a naked flame, she was drawn towards it.

She'd meant to knock on the door, but instead she stopped short. Joe was sitting cross-legged in front of the fire, dressed in just a pair of boxer shorts and a T-shirt. A slow, thoughtful set of movements set the muscles of his back and shoulders rippling beneath the thin fabric, like the movement of a stream running over smooth, water-worn boulders.

Despite his bulk, he was supple. Neve doubted whether her own spine could take that degree of rotation. She swallowed hard, trying not to think about how it might feel to be tangled in the strong, demanding, grace of his body.

Then she saw the scars. She'd expected the ones on his leg, a long surgical scar, together with a deep jagged gash where the break must have occurred. His left arm came as a shock, though. A wide, dark mark running up from his elbow and disappearing beneath the sleeve of his T-shirt. Another, thinner this time and bearing the faint marks of stitches, on his forearm. She caught her breath, stuffing her hand into her mouth to stop herself from crying out.

She should go. Keep her tears for him for somewhere else. Neve was pretty sure that Joe would have no time for them.

'Why don't you come in?' His voice was low, and he didn't turn to meet her gaze.

'I…I'm sorry.' She hissed the words in a whisper. 'I didn't mean to…interrupt you.'

He twisted round to face her. 'You didn't. I was just stretching, and I'm finished now.'

There was no way she could turn her back on him and walk away. No way in the world. Neve padded into the room, closing the door behind her. It seemed somehow wrong to sit on the higher level of the sofa and look down at him, and there was plenty of room to sit down on the quilt, where she could face him.

'This helps? Your leg…'

'Yeah.'

'It's…a nasty injury. Once you leave the hospital, the after-care is…' She ground to a halt. She was babbling anyway. Searching desperately for something to say.

He ran his fingers along his arm, pressing hard, as if the scars might rub off in his hand. They didn't. They were there, and Neve couldn't unsee what she'd seen. Wouldn't have done so for the world.

'You can ask.' He shrugged slightly. 'Or maybe you already know some of it.'

She was about to protest that she knew nothing, that she hadn't been thinking and drawing conclusions. But that would insult his intelligence. 'You're a doctor, aren't you? You were in the army and…' She waved a finger at his arm. 'I guess that you were injured.'

The flash of surprise in his eyes told her that Joe hadn't reckoned that she'd seen quite so much. Then he nodded. 'Royal Canadian Medical Service. How did you work it out?'

'I heard…from someone…that you'd been in the army.'

'Village gossip?'

'Yes. And you said you had medical training and…' She shrugged. 'I can't explain it, I just recognised the way you acted around Michael and Charlie.'

He shook his head, as if that was something he'd feared hearing. 'I guess you can't leave these things behind.'

'Why would you?' Neve couldn't imagine leaving being a doctor behind. It was her reason to get up in the morning. The one piece of her identity that her ex-husband hadn't managed to strip from her.

'It's not what I do any more.'

'Why not?'

A flash of defiance in his eyes. He seemed about to tell her to go away and mind her own business, and then his expression softened. 'My contract of service with the army expired a couple of weeks after I was injured and I didn't re-enlist. It took a while to recover, and I'd done some thinking in the meantime.'

Which didn't go anywhere close to answering the question. Neve tried another. 'How were you hurt?'

'An ambush. I don't remember all the details.'

Most people started off with what they did remember, not what they didn't. It was as if not remembering was Joe's primary purpose.

'You had other injuries? Apart from your leg?'

He nodded. 'Ruptured spleen, partial kidney failure. Abrasions, lacerations…' He reeled off the list with a kind of detachment that Neve recognised. Designed to insulate you from the pain. 'Broke three fingers.'

He was holding up his right hand, flexing the fingers,

and Neve noticed that one bent at a slightly different angle from the others. Somehow the crooked finger brought the horror of the rest of his injuries into sharp focus. Neve began to feel slightly sick.

'I guess it's not unusual. Not being able remember something like that.' She was struggling to keep the tears away. Wanting to convince herself that he'd been spared the trauma of those memories, even though she didn't believe it for a moment.

'No, it's not unusual.' He reached forward, and before she could flinch back he'd brushed a tear from her cheek. 'You don't want to do that. I'll be thinking that it's okay to feel sorry for myself any moment now.'

'And that would never do?'

'No, it wouldn't.' He shot her a look of rebuke. 'It's amazing what modern medicine and a good health package can do. It may not be very pretty, but everything works now.'

'It's...' Neve was suddenly lost for words. She'd talked to people about scars a hundred times before. This was different, she wasn't at work now. 'The scars aren't what I notice about you, Joe.'

He raised one eyebrow in an expression of disbelief, which melted into a wry smile. 'Thanks.'

If she could only tell him what she saw. The proud tilt of his head, a body that had survived so much and yet remained graceful and strong. Any woman would want him...

Don't go there. Just don't.

'You were really good with Michael today.'

He shrugged. 'I was just helping out. You were the one in control.'

'I feel a bit of an idiot now, telling you what to do.'

'You shouldn't. Michael and Charlie were your patients and it was absolutely right that you should have the final say in their treatment. And, as I said, I don't practise as a doctor any more.'

There was no physical reason for that. Maybe an emotional one? PTSD? Neve couldn't believe that Joe no longer wanted to be a doctor. This afternoon he'd seemed to come alive. She shook her head slowly, not sure what to say.

He puffed out a breath. 'It's my decision, Neve.'

'I respect that.'

He nodded. 'I'd appreciate it if you didn't mention it to anyone else.'

'No, of course not. It's not up to me to tell anyone.' Without meaning to, she'd found Joe's weak spot. The fault line that, if tested, might spread into a network of cracks, ready to shatter.

'I should go to bed. Let you get some sleep. I'm glad you're okay. I was worried about your leg.' She wanted to reach out and touch him. But Joe was too proud for anything that seemed like sympathy, and right now he seemed too fragile as well.

'Wait.' It was Joe who reached for her.

There was no thought in his mind about trying to make Neve understand his decisions, or chasing away the feelings that had precipitated them. All he knew was that she was a woman, and he was a man. That she was beautiful in the firelight and that he wanted her. Did it need to be any more complicated than that?

Her eyes widened in surprise, but when he pulled her hand up to his lips she didn't resist him. This was the vision he'd held in his head, the one that had made Michael's weight seem like nothing.

'I really should go.' She didn't move.

'Yeah. You should.' Joe reached for her, pulling her close between his outstretched legs. She smelled so nice. Her hair brushed his cheek. Silk against his stubble.

She turned her mouth up towards his. Waiting. He let her do just that for a moment and then *he* couldn't wait any longer. Joe kissed her.

Her weight in his arms. Her softness. They were just right. Her lips were just right, too. Curving against his into a smile, which lit her beautiful blue eyes. Teasing him just a little and then giving him what he wanted. Another kiss.

'This isn't the place...' She ran her fingers lightly along the line of his jaw.

'No. You're quite right.' Joe kissed her again.

'Or the time...' She kissed him back.

'No, it's not the time either.'

'And there are about a hundred other reasons why I ought to go to my room.' Her little sigh of regret sent a thrill through Joe's already inflamed senses.

'Probably two.'

She turned her gaze onto him. Pensive, gorgeous, and enough to break him into a thousand pieces if she took it into her head to do so. 'Goodnight.'

Every bone in his body ached for her. Neve was the kind of woman who could get a reaction out of a stone, and Joe let her go.

She left him with the taste of one last kiss on his lips and a hunger that no amount of work on his taut muscles was going to calm. One last flash of emotion from her lovely eyes and then she closed the door quietly behind her. Joe flopped onto his back in front of the fire, his hands covering his face. What in the world was he going to do now?

Neve heard the sounds of voices outside the house and rolled over in bed, covering her head with the thick, warm duvet. Just a few moments more. A couple of minutes to persuade herself that she could still taste Joe's kisses on her lips.

Last night her wakefulness had been punctuated by

dreams of him. Holding her, kissing her. Dreams that had turned into nightmares, stark images of Joe broken and bleeding. When she slid out of bed and walked to the window it was almost a surprise to see him in one piece, clearing the snow from his car with the usual powerful grace that characterised all his movements.

By the time she got to the kitchen, the newly charged battery had been secured in the car and had jolted the engine into life. Breakfast was made, and Neve noted with satisfaction that little Daniel's cough was much better today. Then they thanked Daryl and Nancy, and took their leave of them.

Alone in the car, it was as if nothing had changed. Joe was the kind of old-fashioned gentleman who opened doors, carried bags, and it seemed that extended to not mentioning the indiscretions of the night before to anyone, not even the willing co-conspirator in those indiscretions. The kisses, which had made the world a different place this morning, were hidden behind his relaxed, watchful reserve. Along with the scars. Along with all the other things that Neve dared not ask about.

'If we stop by at yours, then I can take you on to Lemister for your surgery. I'll go home, and you can pop in when you've finished.'

'Yes, thanks. I could do with a change of clothes before I take on the morning. And some more coffee.'

Joe chuckled. 'I'll make the coffee.'

Joe closed the front door of his cottage, took off his coat and slung it onto the sofa, ignoring it when it slid off the cushions and onto the floor. He hadn't slept much last night and had watched the feeble rays of the morning sun creep into the room, shedding light on a situation that was already clear to him.

He'd thought that he could remain detached from the

medical side of things. With any other doctor he might have stood a chance, but Neve… She was beautiful, committed and she reminded him of all the reasons he'd become a doctor in the first place. He wanted to be back in that world. And he wanted her.

Joe shook his head. If a broken leg and a few scars were all there was to it, it would have been easy. Not easy perhaps, but he could have beaten the emotional and physical trauma. But the terrible guilt, after a woman had died needlessly on his operating table, was a different matter. The family's grief, which had turned to anger, and the beating that had followed that had seemed like a kind of justice.

No one who made those kinds of mistakes deserved the title of doctor. It was as simple as that. And Joe could wish as hard as he liked that he could turn back time. He couldn't, and that was all there was to it. Taking the stairs two at a time, he made for his bedroom.

'You're not allowed in here.' Joe frowned at the little black cat curled up on the bed, and Almond took no notice. She knew she wasn't allowed in the bedroom, and chose to ignore that fact whenever the door could be pushed open by applying her weight to the bottom corner of it.

'All right, then.' He tickled Almond's neck and she rolled over for more. 'Guess you want some breakfast.'

When he'd started working with Neve, Joe had made an arrangement with his cleaning lady to leave food out for Almond every afternoon, in case he was late home. It had turned out to be a wise piece of forward planning. There was still some food and water left in Almond's bowls, and Joe washed and refilled them, setting them back down on the kitchen floor. Then went upstairs again, to pull off his clothes and scowl at himself in the bathroom mirror.

'Stupid…' The hissed word provoked a yowl from behind him. Almond had a habit of following him wherever he went, and Joe had got used to watching his feet for her. 'Not you, Almond. I'm the one that's the idiot.'

An idiot who was feeling rough around the edges from lack of sleep, and whose head hurt from thinking about all the things he knew he couldn't have. He turned on the shower, and Almond retreated behind a towel that drooped from the rail.

What had made him think that Neve would want him anyway? When he turned, the mirror reminded him of the dark welt that curved across his shoulder and down his back, the scars on his side and arm. The short, jagged scar across his temple, usually hidden by his hair unless he slicked it back or decided on a buzz cut. The list went on. He was damaged goods. And although he seldom stopped to consider it these days, he looked like damaged goods as well.

Joe decided to leave the shower until later. Neve would be a couple of hours, and that was time enough to work some of this nonsense out of his system. A strenuous work-out was what he needed. That, and not dwelling on the way that Neve wrinkled her nose slightly when she smiled.

CHAPTER SIX

JOE'S COTTAGE WAS at the other end of the high street from the church hall, one of a row of three. When the front door opened, a small black cat appeared from behind his legs, dabbing one paw delicately on the ice and then retreating back to claw at the leg of his jeans. He bent to pick the animal up, and it dug its claws into his dark, hooded sweatshirt and started to purr.

He was clean-shaven, his hair slicked back and still a little wet from the shower. Somehow the tiny animal, tucked against his chest accentuated the breadth of his shoulders.

'Come in.' The front door opened straight into a small, comfortable sitting room, and he ushered her inside.

It was a nice room. Old beams across the ceiling contrasted with pale paintwork. There was a little brick fireplace, and a TV was tucked in the corner, dwarfed by piles of books. A brightly coloured armchair and an old leather sofa.

'What's its name?' She wanted to touch Joe, but she wasn't sure how he'd react to that. Instead, Neve crooked her finger and held it out to the cat, who sniffed at it and then allowed her to fondle her neck.

'*Her* name is Almond.' He grinned. 'When I first got her, someone said that she was as sweet as a nut. She's a

Yorkshire cat, so I guess that a Yorkshire expression will do for her.'

'Actually, I think you'll find that expression is used all over England.'

He shrugged. 'Well, she's an English cat, then.'

'So she had to be Almond, or Hazel or…Pea…?'

He chuckled. There was something about the flex of his body, his wet hair and the scent of soap on his skin that spoke of exercise and then a shower.

'Have we got time for some lunch?' His voice cut through Neve's sudden vision of taut muscles, sheened with sweat. 'I'm starving…'

'Yeah. I called Maisie and there are no visits for this afternoon. Apparently the off-roading club has got involved with the driving and the other doctors can easily cover the rest of today so we've got the afternoon off.'

He nodded, seemingly in no hurry to take her home. 'Lunch it is, then.'

He'd led the way through to the kitchen extension at the back of the house and was staring at the contents of the refrigerator when the phone rang. Joe frowned at the instrument then clearly decided that answering it wasn't going to be too much of an interruption.

'At least it's not yours. I don't get those *drop everything and come quick* calls any more.' He picked up the receiver and barked his name down the line, in an unmistakeable invitation to keep it short.

'Edie…?' His gaze left Neve, and he suddenly began to concentrate on the call. 'What's up?'

'Cough mixture…? Yes, of course I'll fetch some, but don't you think you'd better see the doctor?'

He stiffened, holding the phone away from his ear, as an incomprehensible stream of invective sounded from the other end of the line.

'That's as may be, Edie. I'm bringing the doctor round

to see you.' He listened again. 'No, actually you don't have much choice. Just grin and bear it.'

He chuckled, and then put the phone down, turning to Neve.

'Who was that? Did I hear mention of the word "doctor"?'

'Yeah. I'm really sorry about this, but it's Edie Wilcox. She says she's got a terrible cough, and she doesn't sound too good. She doesn't want to see the doctor.'

'So we're going round there?'

He nodded, grinning. 'Yeah. Thanks.'

He picked up a couple of energy bars from the top of the refrigerator, handing her one and tearing into his own while he put his coat on. Picking up her bag, he held the front door open for her.

'After you, Dr Harrison.'

'I hear you did a few jobs for Edie.' She had to walk fast to keep up with Joe.

'Yeah. She can be a bit ferocious, but the trick is to show no fear...' He turned into a tiny front garden, the steps and front path edged with a secure, workmanlike handrail.

'Right. Gotcha.'

Edie took a long time to answer the doorbell, and when she did she was wearing a heavy coat over a nightdress and slippers. She was a tiny, birdlike woman, with bright, sunken eyes and flushed cheeks. Joe stepped forward, holding out his hand.

'I...don't need...'

'I know.' Joe's arm extended protectively around her back, not touching her but there in case she faltered. He guided her into the small, neat sitting room, and she sat down heavily in an easy chair.

'All I need is some cough mixture. And a dash of brandy.' Edie's words were full of bravado, but her eyes told a different story. They were fixed on Joe, almost pleading that he stay.

'Sure you do. But will you do me a favour and let the doctor have a look at you first?'

Edie nodded. 'You're fussing, Joe.'

'That's right. You know Dr Harrison?'

'No.' Edie shot Neve a hostile look and Neve remembered Joe's words. Show no fear.

'Mrs Wilcox.' Neve stepped forward confidently, holding out her hand. 'I'm Neve.'

'Nice to meet you, Dr Harrison.' Edie tightened her lips. Obviously a lady who needed to know you for at least ten years before she'd deign to call you by your first name. Unless, of course, you happened to be Joe.

That was fine. Pulling herself up to her full height, Neve shot Edie a firm look. 'I'd like to take a look at your chest, if that's all right with you.'

Edie folded her arms across her, pulling the coat closed. 'If you say so, Doctor.'

'I'll go and make a cup of tea.' Joe began to retreat.

'Don't you make a mess in my kitchen.' Edie rapped out the words like a command, but her face had softened when she'd looked at him.

'I'll put everything back where it was…' Joe's voice came from the hallway, and Neve closed the door behind him.

'You're the doctor that Joe's been driving.' Edie wasn't going to submit herself to an examination before Neve had given a full account of herself.

'Yes, that's right. I couldn't have managed without his help this past week.'

'He didn't bring my shopping until half past eight the day before yesterday.' Edie tightened her lips, as if shopping in the evenings was another thing she didn't particularly approve of.

Neve suppressed a smile. 'We didn't finish until seven that day.' Joe had made no mention that he would be doing Edie's shopping, and Neve had supposed he would go straight home. But, then, the more she found out about Joe, the more she realised just how much she didn't know.

Edie gave a little nod. 'He's a good man.'

'Yes, he is.'

That settled, Edie relaxed her grip on her coat enough to allow Neve to examine her. 'I hope you're going to warm that up.' Edie was looking at her stethoscope as if it were an instrument of torture. 'Dr Johnstone never does.'

Neve knew for a fact that the avuncular, friendly senior partner of the practice *always* warmed the diaphragm of his stethoscope before placing it on a patient's skin. She let that go and handed the instrument to Edie.

'Here. Hold the end in your hand for a moment to warm it, while I take your temperature.'

Joe took his time making the tea. Edie's stubbornness could be immoveable at times but, then, Neve's smile was irresistible. Somehow he didn't give much for Edie's chances.

He didn't give a great deal for his own either. He'd thought about coming up with an excuse that would make him temporarily unavailable to accompany Neve, ending their relationship there, but he'd made a promise and he wouldn't go back on that. In any case, the idea of another volunteer encroaching on what he now saw as his territory was unthinkable.

Like it or not, Joe knew he would see it through to the end. He heaved a sigh, placing cups and saucers precisely onto a tray. He waited before pouring the hot water from the kettle into the pot, knowing that Edie would complain if the tea was stewed. Joe found some biscuits in the scullery and tried to divert himself by arranging them in different patterns on a plate.

When he heard Neve's footsteps in the hall, he set the kettle to boil again. She was smiling. His brain—or maybe his heart—took special note every time she smiled.

'Edie wants to know what you're doing. She says that your grandmother would be horrified at the way you make tea.'

Slowly, irrevocably, Neve was beginning to turn his world upside down and make him doubt every part of his carefully constructed life here. When she was around he had to remember to stop grinning like a fool, staring like a moonstruck child. 'She must be feeling all right, then.'

'She's got a nasty cold, but she'll be all right in a few days.'

'Her chest's clear?' Joe wondered whether that might be misconstrued as fussing. Or a comment on how thorough Neve had been in her examination.

'Yes. But it would be good to keep an eye on her.'

'She has a daughter in the village. I'll give her a call.'

'Good.' She turned her attention to the tea things. 'Edie told me to remind you to warm the pot.'

He rolled his eyes. 'Edie's mission in life is to teach me how to make a decent cup of tea.'

'And has she?'

He shrugged, laughing. 'I'm a work in progress. She did mention once that my tea wasn't too bad. I think she wasn't feeling up to much that day.'

'Well, I'll leave you to concentrate, then. I'm just going to wash my hands.'

Neve had obviously made the mistake of leaving her stethoscope lying around, because when Joe walked into the sitting room Edie had the instrument plugged into her ears and was listening to the chest of her old ginger cat.

Clearly she was feeling better and her irrepressible interest in life was resurfacing. He put the tray down and tapped her on the shoulder.

'If you put it there, all you'll hear is Errol digesting his breakfast.'

Edie didn't reply but moved the diaphragm of the stethoscope. She listened intently and then nodded. 'Well, he's alive. Not that you'd know it. He hasn't moved recently.'

Joe grinned. 'And what did the doctor say? Are *you* alive?'

Edie gave him one of her looks. Most people seemed to think that Edie's glare could fry you on the spot, but Joe was somehow immune to it. Perhaps because he got her sense of humour.

'She says that you've been fussing. Sit down, you're making the place look untidy.'

Joe sat. Edie asked for no quarter, and gave none. She'd never referred to his injuries, other than to nod approvingly when he'd thrown the walking stick away and expect him to carry her shopping. She was pure gold.

'Nice girl. Pretty, too.' Edie lost interest in the stethoscope, having learned everything she could from it, and turned her attention to Joe.

'Yes. Only she's not really a girl...'

'None of them are these days.' Edie seemed to have regained the rest of her usual feistiness. She might talk tough, but underneath it all she'd been feeling ill and worried and Neve had obviously seen that and put her mind at rest. 'And I may be old, but I'm not blind.'

'I can see that.' Joe grinned at her.

'Don't try getting around me, Joseph Lamont. Try that smile with her instead.'

'I don't know what you mean.'

'Yes, you do.' Edie waved an imperious finger at the tray. 'Did you warm the pot?'

'I did.'

'Then perhaps it'll be drinkable.' Humour sliced the faded blue of Edie's eyes. 'I won't have a biscuit just yet. Don't want to spoil that pretty pattern you've made until she's seen it.'

Edie's daughter had arrived and ordered her upstairs to bed in no-nonsense tones that bore a remarkable resemblance to those of her mother. Neve packed up her things, flashing a querying look in Joe's direction when she found a ginger cat hair on her stethoscope, but he just shrugged with a look of mock innocence. Then they were ready to go.

'Lunch?'

'Sounds good.' Neve had rather hoped that Joe hadn't forgotten he'd promised her lunch.

'How about the pub? It's nothing fancy…'

Nothing fancy was just what Neve wanted at the moment. 'Sounds perfect.'

They tramped towards the painted sign, which showed a white deer, its breast pierced by an arrow. 'I'm told this is the oldest building in the village.' He grinned at her.

'You've heard the story too?'

'Oh, yes.' He grinned. 'King Henry VIII took time off from a royal progress to do some hunting in the area, and *The Bleeding Hart* was named to celebrate that. In the summer it's crammed with tourists.'

'But you're a local now?'

'I've moved around so much that it only takes a couple of weeks before I reckon I'm local…' Joe shrugged. 'As far as everyone else is concerned, I'm working on it.'

He ducked through the low doorway, and led the way to the bar. Beamed ceilings, slightly sloping walls and an eclectic furnishing style gave the impression that the place had been here since the year dot, and the soot-scarred fireplace attested to a succession of roaring fires, just like the one that blazed there now.

'A pint, thanks, Mark.' Joe indicated the tap that bore the insignia of the local bitter and turned to Neve. 'What'll you have?'

She leaned across the bar, squinting at the chalked board above Mark's head. 'Hot punch sounds good.'

Mark nodded and Joe handed her a menu. 'What are you having?'

'Shepherd's pie. Runner beans, carrots and…' She turned to him, unable to make a decision. 'I suppose chips on the side is a bit much.'

'They do very good chips here.' Joe grinned.

Neve's ex-husband had always ordered for her when they'd gone out to eat, taking it on himself to watch her waistline when he did so. It appeared that Joe had no such concerns, and if she wanted to resist temptation, she was going to have to do it all by herself.

'No…I won't have chips. I'll have apple pie to follow. With cream.' She was reaching inside her coat, but Joe had the better start. He signalled to Mark to make it two of everything and handed him the money, waving away the note she proffered from her purse.

'Thanks. My treat next time.'

'I'll look forward to it.' Joe grinned and picked up the drinks, navigating past the clusters of chairs and tables to a seat by the fire.

'So how did you get to know Edie Wilcox?' Neve took a sip of her punch and nodded in approval.

'She gave me the evil eye a couple of times when I first got here. Looked as if she might kick the crutches out from under me. The first time she spoke to me was in the village shop. She took one look at me, pointed to the chair by the counter and told me to sit down because I was making the place look untidy.'

Neve snorted with laughter. 'And did you?'

'Yeah. I was fed up with everyone back home wrapping me up in cotton wool, and I'd had about as much sympathy as I could take. Edie never gave me a shred of it.' He took a draught of his beer.

'But she looked out for you?'

'Oh, yes. She goes to the village shop every morning, and before I knew it she was expecting me to walk her down there and back, nice and slowly because of her bad leg. Funnily enough, as soon as I started to be able to walk a bit faster, her bad leg got miraculously better.'

'She had your measure, then.' Neve chuckled.

'Is it that hard?'

'Don't know. Is it?' A now-familiar tingle registered at the back of her neck. Danger? Pleasure? A bit of both?

'There isn't that much to know.' Joe took another draught of his beer. 'You've heard it already.'

'Really?' She raised one eyebrow, just to show that she didn't quite believe him. He nodded, as if he was perfectly aware of that but there was nothing he could do about it.

'Yeah. Really.'

There was no shortage of things to talk about over lunch, or afterwards when he took her home. Village gossip, the weather. The price of apples. All the things that didn't really matter all that much. Neve reflected that Joe must want it that way.

They were caught in a no man's land somewhere between friends and lovers. Not wanting to go back, not daring to go forward.

'I'll see you tomorrow, then.' Neve made no move to get out of the car, but sat staring at her front door.

'Yeah. Same time?'

'That would be great, thanks.'

For a moment she thought that he might reach for her.

Maybe she ought to give him some sign. He couldn't know that the constant craving for his scent, his skin had given him the right to hold her. It had given him the right to break her front door down, carry her upstairs and do pretty much anything he pleased.

'Right.' Suddenly he swung out of the car, fetching her bags from the back seat and carrying them up the front path. Neve followed, her steps slowed by indecision, waiting for him to make the first move. Wondering whether she should.

He dumped her bags on the front doorstep and turned, striding back to the car. The grin that he shot her from the driving seat ought to have lost some of its potency at this distance but somehow didn't. Then the car began to recede slowly away, down the snow-filled lane.

CHAPTER SEVEN

THE RING OF the doorbell synchronised perfectly with the time pips for eight o'clock on the radio. Almost as if he'd been waiting, at the other end of the lane, to time his arrival. Neve decided to enquire no further. Enquiring no further seemed to be exactly what Joe wanted.

He seemed more relaxed this morning, less restless. He wished her a cheery good morning and they took the road that wound its way to Cryersbridge, through the village, and to the nursing home on the other side, drawing up in the wide, snow-filled drive.

'You should come inside.' He hadn't moved to get out of the car when they came to a halt. 'I'll be a while, I've a few people to see here and there are some things I've promised to do for the district nurse. You'll freeze out here.'

He nodded, getting out of the car without a word. The manager of the nursing home waved to them from the window, and a wall of heat hit Neve when she opened the door and ushered them inside.

'Dr Harrison, thanks for coming. The surgery said you'd be here this morning, but I wasn't expecting you until later.'

'I had some help. This is Joe Lamont, he's been driving me for the last week. Joe, this is Jane Matthews.'

Joe's smile turned the warmth of Jane's up a notch.

'They're still serving breakfast in the dining room. Go and get yourself a cup of tea and sit in the lounge if you'd like.'

The invitation wasn't all just good hospitality. Neve imagined that the residents hadn't received too many visitors in the last few days, and a new face was always welcome.

He turned a look of untrammelled pleasure onto Jane, as if she'd just invited him to the Queen's garden party. 'Thanks, I'd like that.'

'Good.' Jane looked around quickly and, finding no one available to show him the way, pointed to her left. 'The dining room is through there, you can't miss it. Just introduce yourself…'

'Sure.' Joe turned quickly, and strode away in the direction of Jane's pointing finger.

'Is that it, then?' Neve had seen six of the residents, redressed a leg ulcer, and made sure that the various bumps, wheezes and an unexplained watery eye were nothing serious and could be managed here.

'There's Stuart. Dr Johnstone usually sees him…'

'Ah, yes. Fairly new resident, became very distressed when he moved here. Dr Johnstone has him on a mild antidepressant. How's he been?'

'Much better. He's joining in with some of the activities now. Still keeps himself to himself, but some people prefer that.' Jane grinned. 'He has good days and bad, but on balance the good ones are getting more frequent.'

'Okay. I'll find a quiet corner and have a chat with him.'

'Great. Thanks.' Jane led the way back to the main sitting room, scanning the circle of faces from the doorway.

'Hallie, have you seen Stuart, love?' Jane's teenaged daughter had obviously been pressed into service while the home was short-staffed, and was dispensing tea and biscuits from a trolley.

'In the small sitting room, I think.' Hallie leaned towards her mother. 'With the new guy. Who is he?' One look at the grin on Hallie's face told Neve that she was referring to Joe.

'Don't get your hopes up, he'll be gone soon. He's driving Dr Harrison today.'

Hallie wrinkled her nose, and shot Neve a look of undisguised envy. Suddenly, seventeen seemed a very long time and a whole world of complications away.

The small sitting room was bathed in light. The high windows caught the best of the morning sun, reflecting off the snow outside, and the room was bright and warm. Joe was sitting in an armchair, next to a wiry, neatly dressed elderly man, whose lined, weather-beaten face attested to a lifetime spent outdoors.

'What did you do, then?' Joe's face was alive with interest, and Neve hung back in the doorway, waiting to see how Stuart would respond to him.

'Pulled 'er out wi' a tractor. But that road through the fells is always like that in winter. Summat to do with the way the wind blows. The snow just piles up through there.' Stuart leaned forward, tracing his finger across the map in front of them.

'And what about here?' Joe indicated another spot on the map, about a mile south.

Stuart's face became suddenly confused. 'Depends.' Uncertain anger sounded in his voice. The notes had stated that Stuart had mild dementia, and his reaction was typical. He was lashing out at Joe before he'd admit that he couldn't remember.

Joe didn't miss a beat. No surprise, no trying to get Stuart to explain. Just what Neve would have expected from a doctor who was sensitive to his patients' feelings as well as their medical needs. 'Yeah, I guess so. Probably best not to risk it. I'm thinking that going this way is the thing to do. It's further but more sheltered.'

Stuart looked carefully at the map. It was difficult to say whether he was really following Joe's line of thought, but that didn't matter. Joe had neatly skirted the lapse in memory, and Stuart's self-respect remained intact.

'Yes. That way's sheltered. That way's best.'

Joe nodded. 'Yeah. Thanks, Stuart, that's good to know.'

'Seventy years on the land, in all sorts of weather. You pick up a few things.' Stuart was no longer a frail old man who wasn't of much use to anyone. 'I'd take you myself, but…'

'You've done your share, mate.' There was respect in Joe's voice but no pity.

'That I have.' Stuart nodded sagely. 'That thing over there's crooked.' A sudden change of subject, as different thoughts jostled for supremacy in Stuart's mind.

'The tree?' Joe followed Stuart's gaze towards the brightly decorated Christmas tree in the corner of the room.

'No, the star on the top. The girls can't reach it…'

Joe took the hint. Striding over to the tree, he reached up and adjusted the star. 'Better…?'

'That'll do.' Stuart suddenly seemed to realise that Neve was in the room. 'Who's this?'

Joe looked round and caught Neve staring at him. 'It's the doctor. Looks like I've got to go now.' He collected his map from the coffee table and held out his hand to shake Stuart's. 'Thanks for all the advice.'

'No trouble. I seem to be always here now, if there's anything else you want to know.'

'Thanks, Stuart. I'll know where to find you.'

Joe had already done what Neve was here to do. Get Stuart talking, without making it too obvious that she was here to assess his mood and how much he could remember. She sat down next to the elderly man.

'I'm just here to have a chat. Why don't you stay a moment, Joe?'

She thought that the look she shot him implied that the invitation to stay was anything but casual. If Joe could talk some more to Stuart, and she could just listen, that would probably answer all the questions she had. But Joe, it appeared, had other ideas.

'I've got to go and clear the snow from the car.' He grinned at Stuart. 'Kick the tyres...'

Stuart nodded. 'What have you got fitted?'

'High silica snow tyres. I don't know what everyone around here has against snow tyres, no one seems to fit them. They're standard practice in Canada.'

Stuart chuckled. 'You need a tractor, boy. Get over anything.'

'I dare say. Bit chilly for my passengers, though.' He gave Stuart a parting smile, and then he was gone.

She was obviously angry. Neve was having difficulty marching in two feet of snow, but her face was a picture as she toiled across to the car. Pink with exertion, her lips pressed together in a sure sign of emotion, she was intoxicating. He twisted the ignition key, trying to keep his mind away from those thoughts. The engine almost choked into life and then died.

'Thanks for that.' Joe expressed his wry gratitude to the treacherous gods of fate. If he tried again too soon he'd flood the engine so he was going to have to leave it now and sit with her for a few awkward minutes in the car.

He got out of his seat and opened the tailgate so she could put her bag inside.

'Car won't start?' She turned her lovely blue eyes up towards him, trying to catch his gaze. There was more than a hint of fire in them, which made him want to kiss her.

'Give it a minute. It'll start.'

She nodded and walked to the passenger door, getting in before Joe could close the tailgate and get around there to open the door for her. As she wished. He trudged back to the driver's door, kicked a minuscule shard of ice from one of the tyres in an attempt to put the awkward moment off, and then got into the car.

Her hands were clasped in her lap and she was staring straight ahead, as if assessing the road in front of her. Joe wondered if he should get out and clear the windscreen again.

'You might have stayed.'

Yes, he might have. But that wasn't what he did any more.

'I had to come out here and get the car started.'

'Right.' She turned her gaze onto him, bright and angry, and it rocked him to the very core of his being. 'Go on, then.'

'Give it a minute. I don't want to flood the engine.'

She frowned at him. It seemed that he wasn't going to get off the hook that easily. A part of him embraced that, aching for more, and Joe wondered again if he hadn't been living the quiet life a little too long.

'You're Stuart's doctor. It wasn't appropriate for me to hang around.'

'Why don't you let me be the judge of that? I wasn't asking you to do a full-blown assessment of him, just to keep him talking a little while longer.'

'And you're not capable to talking to someone?' Joe was in no doubt that Neve had handled Stuart with compassion and sensitivity. What he couldn't fathom was why she had seemed so set on dragging him in to help.

'Of course I'm capable of talking to him. I could ask him the questions if you think that's going to do any good.'

The standard set of questions, things that everyone was supposed to know, which were designed to assess dementia patents. It was likely that Stuart had come across them before, and he might recall their purpose. If he knew why Neve was asking the questions but couldn't remember the answers, it was just setting him up for failure and humiliation.

'You didn't, did you?' Concern for Stuart snagged at him, and then he remembered that this was Neve he was talking to. Of course she hadn't. 'I'm not sure *I* know who the prime minister is over here…'

The temperature in the car shot up. 'Stop being a smart-arse, of course I didn't. But the map and his local knowledge were a great way to get him talking and assess what he remembers.'

That hadn't been Joe's intention, he'd just fallen into conversation with Stuart and had recognised the frustration of a man who felt that he was no longer of any use to anyone. It had been the act of a human being, not a doctor. But the knowledge that Neve was right cut him to the bone.

'Look, we both have a job to do. We don't have to be overjoyed about it, but we need each other right now. So let's just get on with it, shall we?'

She flushed red. 'Okay, so I need you. Is that what you want me to say? I'm not quite sure how you need me…'

Joe wasn't sure quite why he needed her either. Other than that the air seemed thin, almost unbreathable when she wasn't there. There was an insistent rapping on the misted car window beside him and Neve jumped.

The window slid down, and he saw Hallie outside, shivering in just a blouse and cardigan. 'Stuart says to pump the accelerator. You'll need to start in second gear.' She turned, without waiting for an answer, and skittered back to the warmth of the house.

He already knew that, but he wasn't going to deprive Stuart of his moment of glory. He gave a wave to the figure at the window, twisted the ignition key and the engine growled into life. A quick thumbs-up in Stan's direction and they were ready to go.

'Where next?'

'Straight through the village then take the first left. There's a house about two hundred yards down.' She seemed to have made the same decision as him. Arguments about who did what, and why, were sheer self-indulgence. They needed to save their energy for the road ahead.

CHAPTER EIGHT

SILENCE HAD GIVEN way to frosty formality and then to studied good manners. By the time they drew up outside Neve's house the day had worn them both down, and a couple of smiles that weren't strictly necessary had passed between them.

'I've been thinking…' Neve took a breath. Letting Joe drive away without clearing the air between them had become impossible.

'Yeah?' He leaned back in his seat, stretching his legs as much as the footwell would allow. Cautious. Watchful as ever.

She'd better make the admission now, before she lost her nerve. 'I was angry.'

Joe grinned. 'Now tell me something I don't know.'

All right. This was a different way of handling it. Not quite the way her ex-husband had approached anything that even approximated disagreement on Neve's part but, then, the one thing that didn't seem to register with Joe was her mistakes.

'I'm sorry.' It was easier to apologise when an apology wasn't demanded.

'No, you were right. I might not practise, but that doesn't absolve me from being a human being. Staying around and chatting to Stuart was what anyone would have done.'

Joe had clearly been thinking too. Coming around to her way of seeing things. It was a novel experience.

'Come in and have some tea.'

'You're tired.' The look that ignited in his eyes told her that Joe was wondering the same as she was. Whether tea was the only thing he was supposed to be coming in for. The thought of Joe's embrace, testing her to the brink of exhaustion, flooded through her senses.

'I'd like some company.'

He reached forward and found her hand. When he pulled her glove off, it felt as if he was undressing her. He laid his gentle fingers around hers, and it was as if they were naked already. Neve leaned forward, brushing her lips against his.

The suddenness of his next move activated his seat belt, and for a moment he was pinned against the seat. Cursing, he punched the release, twisting round and pulling her into his arms. Sudden heat jolted through her when he kissed her.

'Come inside.' The gear shift was in the way, and the steering-wheel wouldn't allow him to get as close as she'd like. Their clothes wouldn't allow him to get as close as she'd like.

'If I let you go…?'

'You're going to have to. One step back and two steps forward.'

His lips curved against hers. 'I like the way you think…'

She liked the way he thought as well. There was no rushing up the front path, struggling with her keys. He opened the front gate for her, his hand on her back while she opened the front door. Treating her as if she was something precious. He would ask, but he didn't just go ahead and take.

As soon as they were inside, she wound her arms around his neck, pulling him down for another kiss. She felt his hands around her hips, lifting her upwards and against his body, and she wound her legs around his waist, just making it clear, if either of them was in any doubt, what was coming next.

Separated by layers of high-performance down and waterproofing, she couldn't feel the lines of his body. All she could feel was his strength, supporting her weight, crushing her close until she couldn't breathe.

'Upstairs…' She took just enough time out from kissing him for that one word.

'I *really* like the way you think.' The curve of his body was urgent against hers, but he seemed intent on taking his time. 'I want to undress you. Piece by piece.'

Just the thought made her head swim. 'Go on…'

'And then I want to touch your skin.' He nuzzled against her neck, his breath caressing her ear. 'Fingers… Then lips…'

This was too much. If he didn't stop asking and start doing, she was going to faint. 'Upstairs. Now, Joe.'

She unwound herself from him, difficult though it was, then led him up the stairs and into her freezing-cold bedroom. Went to flip on the light and Joe caught her wrist before she could do so, pressing her fingers against his lips. In the darkness she felt him pull off her coat and then the padded liner, then he walked her backwards until she fell onto the bed. Bending, he pulled her boots off, then her thick woollen socks. She shivered a little in the cold air.

The hall light, filtering in through the half-open doorway, was enough to see his shape. The delicious shadow of his bulk loomed over her, as he hurriedly shed his coat and boots, pulling off his sweater. Then his warmth enfolded her again, and he unbuttoned her thick cardigan. Slid his hands inside, and then pulled it off, along with the sweater she was wearing underneath.

'Joe…' She pulled at his shirt and he dragged it over

his head. Her fingers slid to the button on his jeans and he slipped out of them. It was the fastest she'd seen a guy undress in her life.

'Thermal vest...' His lips were close to her ear again. 'Very practical.'

The way he was taking his time, easing her out of it, exploring every new inch of skin with his fingers, wasn't at all practical. It was a simmering, languid testament to his intentions of taking his time with her.

'Condoms. In the drawer...'

'Later. This is all for you, honey.' Joe was gently slipping her slacks down, kissing the skin on the inside of her leg as he went. His words echoed through her consciousness, like a golden, erotic promise of what was to come.

'What about you...' He silenced her by cupping her breast with his hand, brushing gently against the nipple. All hell broke loose, fire shooting through her body as if it had just been injected straight into a vein.

'You first.' His hand slid around her back, unhooking her bra with an uncommon dexterity. She felt the soft cotton of his T-shirt, brush against her stomach...

'Joe, wait.' It took all her strength to push him away, even though he drew back at the slightest touch of her fingers. Every ounce of her self-control.

'What is it, honey?' She could see the outline of his face in the darkness. Feel his hand, resting lightly on her stomach.

'Not like this, Joe.' He probably hadn't even thought about this. It was just instinct, born of the feeling that his body was broken and disfigured. But he was about to squander their precious first time, rob her of the chance to share it with him.

Neve rolled away from him, leaving him stretched out

on the bed. Stumbling over to the window, she drew the curtains, although there was no one outside. Then she picked the matches up from the mantelpiece, half closing her eyes against the sharp flare of light as she struck one of them.

There were four large candles, standing on the mantelpiece, in front of a huge, heavy framed mirror. As she lit them, light slid across the contours of her body, caressing her curves.

What had he been thinking? Neve felt good, she smelled good and she tasted wonderful. But she looked stunning. Long, slim limbs, beautiful breasts… She was enough to bring a man to his knees.

'That's better, isn't it?'

'You're beautiful.' His voice came out hoarse with emotion. Not like him at all.

'And you…' She sashayed back over to the bed, and climbed onto it. He could see the high brass bedstead now, and the thought of her gripping hard onto the rails nearly destroyed him. 'You are not going to get away with this.'

She rolled him onto his back, sitting astride his stomach. Joe had a horrible feeling he knew what was coming next. She bent over him, running her tongue around the edge of his ear. 'What did you think? That I don't want to see you?'

That had crossed his mind. But largely it had been unthought, an instinctive need to give her pleasure, feel her break in his arms.

'Or did you reckon on making me scream first, before you got rid of this.' She pulled at his T-shirt. 'Maybe I wouldn't notice quite so much then.'

He hugged her close. She seemed to know his intentions better than he did, right now. 'It's a thought. I particularly like the screaming part…'

She giggled against his chest. Clearly she did too. 'Yeah, well there wasn't going to be any screaming because I don't scream in the dark. It's a lonely place, the darkness.'

Suddenly it was. Suddenly the one thing that Joe wanted was for her to see him, all of him, just as he was. Maybe accept him a little.

'So we've got some light. What now?' She might have the courage that he didn't.

She reached over to the bedside table, opening the drawer with one hand, and drawing out a pair of scissors. The blades gleamed in the flickering light.

'Take it off, Joe.'

'Or what?' He tucked his hands behind his head. He'd never had a woman cut his clothes off before. Not when he was fully conscious, anyway. Even that thought didn't break through the depth of his longing.

'This better not be your best T-shirt.' She tugged the hem out from under her, and snipped at it. The sound seemed like the tearing of all his inhibitions. Then the first long cut. He could feel the touch of cold steel against his stomach.

'Careful....' Joe swallowed the words. He knew she wouldn't cut him, and he didn't much care if she did. It was the newly born hope that he so wanted to preserve. And she could destroy it now, with one look.

'You trust me?' She slid her hand under his T-shirt, and he felt her fingers against his skin. Her mouth curved into the most beautiful smile he'd ever seen.

'Yeah. I trust you, honey.'

Carefully, slowly, she cut the T-shirt off him. Stopping to kiss his chest. Making sure that he knew she liked what she saw. More than that. Her body couldn't lie, and she was turned on by what she saw. Joe reached for her with trembling fingers, caressing her, and she cried out.

The scissors clattered onto the floor beside the bed. Her

hands tugged at his boxer shorts, and Joe lifted his hips, so she could pull them off.

'Nice.' She kissed him on the lips. 'Very nice. Very big…'

He held her still on top of him, his hands clasped around her waist. 'That's all because of you…'

'Look…' She forced his head to one side, so he could not longer look straight at her. Then Joe realised that there was another mirror in the room, on top of the dressing table. She must have turned it slightly when she'd got up to light the candles, because instead of sitting straight it was trained right onto the bed. 'What do you see, Joe?'

'You and me…'

'Just that?' She smiled at him in the glass.

'Just that.' Nothing else. Two bodies, both taut and trembling, ready for each other. The scars were still there, but right now they didn't seem to matter.

He pulled her down so he could kiss her breasts. Heard her sigh, so he kept her right there, using his mouth to make her cry out. Once wasn't going to be enough, it never could be, and he kept going until every breath was a moan.

Her whole body was aching for his. She told him that. Neve was unused to telling anyone anything very much in bed, but he'd needed to hear it at first. And then it was like a glorious affirmation, building the heat between them until she felt drops of sweat prickling on her spine.

'What was I thinking?' He whispered the words against her ear. 'I love the feel of your skin against mine and I nearly…'

That didn't matter. Nothing mattered other than one thing. 'Now, Joe. Please…now.'

He flipped her over, with as much effort as it took to turn a page, his body taut and strong against hers. The sound of tearing fabric as he pulled her knickers off only added a delicious twist of urgency. When she felt his fingers, trailing down her belly, parting her legs, she almost blacked out from sheer sexual need. Her body responded almost immediately to his light, deft touch.

He kept the orgasm rolling. Didn't stop, just changed the rhythm. Kissed her, caressing her through the aftershocks and into a deeper need, one that could wait until they'd wrung the last drops of sensation out of each and every moment.

She flung one arm out, reaching for the condoms, and missed the box completely. His longer reach got them, and he tipped the box upside down on the bedside table, catching one of the foil packets up in his fingers.

Neve didn't even notice the break when he put the condom on because he was whispering in her ear. Words of one syllable that made it more than plain what he was about to do. Warm caresses that told her he was going to do it with feeling.

Slowly, he slid inside her. She moved convulsively and he shook his head, letting a little of his weight pin her immobile beneath him. 'Hold up there, sweetheart. I'm not going to manage long and slow if you keep this up.'

His olive skin against her pallor. The muscles of his shoulders and arms flexing as he moved. That conscious hesitation before each caress, which let her feel everything before he even touched her, and then again when he did.

He guided her legs a little higher, settling them around his waist and choking out her name as he did so. He slid his hand around her to the base of her spine and lifted a few inches, thrusting inside her again.

'Oh!' Suddenly the soft, warm pleasure spun into something more urgent. Joe's gaze was on her, watching every reaction, as he changed the angle slightly and thrust again. This time he got things more blissfully, agonisingly right than she had even realised was possible.

* * *

When she came for the second time it was like electricity running down his spine. As if somehow he could feel what she felt by some process of osmosis, or mind-melding, or whatever the hell else it was that seemed to bind their souls together. And then his whole world seemed to disappear into a vortex of wanting her, turning him into a mess of sheer feeling.

It took a conscious effort not to collapse on top of her in the almost overwhelming aftermath. Carefully, shakily he rolled them both over onto their sides, covering her with the duvet, and she snuggled in tight against him.

He let out a sigh of pure contentment. Somehow the most beautiful woman in the world found him attractive. He couldn't account for it, but he wasn't going to argue with it. Maybe, just maybe this could work. He could try to settle, piece together his life. He had made a plan out of having no plan, so far. Maybe that could change.

He was clutching at straws, but straws were all he had right now. He watched her sleep for a while, and when she stirred he watched her wake.

'Hey, you…' She curled her arm around his neck, pulling him in for a kiss. 'How long…?'

'Half an hour. You okay?'

'Better than okay.' She grinned up at him. 'Are you hungry?'

'Yeah I'm hungry. For you…'

She bumped her cheek against his shoulder. Didn't care that it was resting against puckered, scarred flesh. She didn't seem to even notice it. 'What are you, superman?'

'I said I was still hungry. Didn't say I was in any state to do anything about it.'

Neve smiled lazily up at him. He liked the way she could hardly keep her eyes open. She was soft, and warm, and it made him feel good to think that their lovemaking had unravelled her as much as it had him.

'Be sure to let me know when you are.'

He chuckled, smoothing her shining curls back from her brow, and she shifted a little against him until she found a position she liked, her limbs tangled with his. He held her while she drifted off to sleep again.

Later, much later Joe carefully moved her head from his chest and got out of bed. The air was icy cold. He slipped into his jeans and sweater, and made his way downstairs to the kitchen. A quick reconnoitre of the refrigerator, and he decided that bacon sandwiches were just the thing.

When he returned to the bedroom, wafting the scent of the food in her direction, she reacted by wrinkling her nose slightly. Joe smiled to himself, murmuring quietly into her ear.

Her eyes snapped open. 'You, Joe Lamont, are an angel.'

He grinned, putting the plate down on the bedside table and handing her a napkin.

'Take your clothes off…'

'Before or after I pass you a sandwich?' He raised an eyebrow in query.

'Ow…I love bacon sandwiches and I'm so hungry…' She teased him for a moment, then her earnest blue gaze found his. 'Before. I like to see you naked. Unless you have a problem with that?'

Not one. In fact, this was the first time he'd felt anything apart from hesitancy about undressing in the last eighteen months. He took off his sweater and jeans, and she smiled, that beautiful smile that made him feel like a million dollars.

'Better?'

'Much. Bring the sandwiches with you when you come back to bed.…'

CHAPTER NINE

THEY ATE AND TALKED. Drank coffee and talked. Embraced, in the comfort of her bed, which was so much warmer with him in it, and talked.

'I got it at auction. It's old...' He'd asked her about the brass bedstead.

'It's great. Really solid.' He tested his strength against one of the bars.

'Yeah. Took me days to clean up, but I was really pleased with it. You know the auction house just outside Cryers-bridge?' He nodded. 'I got nearly all my furniture there.'

She'd furnished her home with good-quality, second-hand furniture, all restored and polished up to look better than new. It wasn't a low-budget option, it would have been cheaper to buy from a furniture warehouse, but she'd chosen well and the pieces matched the style of the old farmhouse, solid and attractive.

'So...what? You threw away all your old furniture?' She never seemed to talk about what she'd done before she'd come here. She talked about London, her family, her childhood. She talked about medical school, but the years in between then and now hardly seemed to exist for her.

'I was staying with my parents for six months before I moved up here.' She drew the bedcovers around her as if she was suddenly cold.

'And before that?'

Neve obviously had an issue with whatever had come before that. She was almost like a cornered animal, suddenly motionless with terror. But he'd asked now, and dropping the subject wasn't going to make her feel any better. The only thing he could do was make the answer a bit easier. Joe took a wild guess. 'I imagine you probably lived with someone...?'

She nodded, watching his face. 'I was married... There hasn't been anyone for two years...'

A jealous guy, then. In Joe's experience, women didn't get that defensive without some reason.

'I have an admission to make to you, too.' He looked at her with mock solemnity.

'Yes?'

'You're not my first either...'

She was laughing now, and that was just the way he wanted her. Not worrying about what he'd think of her past. History was history, and he was the one holding her tonight.

'You mean you haven't been saving yourself for me?' She nudged at his shoulder playfully. 'I'm disappointed.'

The thought occurred to him that he just might have done, if he'd known. 'No. I've had a girlfriend before... two, maybe.'

'I bet you've had hundreds.' She ran her hand across his chest in a gesture of possessiveness, and he was surprised at how much it pleased him.

He pretended to count on his fingers. 'Not quite that many.'

'Never...married, though?' She almost managed to make the question sound casual.

'No. I moved around a lot.' Joe had never been short of female company, but he'd always put his career first. When that had come crashing down he'd been left with nothing. He reached for her, pulling her against him, the touch of her skin somehow reassuring.

'Are you hungry?' She picked up his arm, looking at his watch. 'It's getting late.'

'Starving. I'll cook for you, if you like.'

She considered the idea. 'You cook?'

'Of course I do. I eat don't I? Trust me, once you've tasted my crème brûlée, you'll be putty in my hands.'

'I wouldn't bank on it.'

'You don't like crème brûlée?'

She tapped one finger on his chest, as if to catch his attention. 'I'm not putty in anyone's hands.'

It had just been a throwaway comment, but she seemed to have taken it seriously. Joe caught her hand, pressing her fingers to his lips in a gesture of goodwill. 'I'll remember that. Although I can't promise that I won't find I'm putty in *your* hands from time to time.'

She ignored the observation. 'And talking about ground rules…'

'Were we?'

'I just…' She sat up in the bed, wrapping one end of the duvet around her body. 'I'm not the clingy type. I really like being with you Joe, but I'm not going to ask you to spend every waking moment with me. You don't have to take responsibility for me.'

Somehow he felt deflated. Joe told himself that this was what he wanted. He was in no position to make any promises to anyone about where he'd be or what he'd be doing in six months' time. But on another level he was upset. He cared for her. He wanted to take care of her, and that entailed a bit more than just meeting up a couple of nights a week for sex. He adjusted the thought slightly. Amazing sex.

'Does that mean I can't cook for you?'

'No, of course not.'

'Or that you can't cook for me?'

'No. I just don't want you to feel that I'm dependent on you…' She shrugged. 'You know.'

No, not really. It had never occurred to Joe that Neve was dependent on him. She was fiercely, gloriously independent, and that was one of the things he respected about her.

'You're worrying about nothing, honey. Aren't things just fine the way they are?'

She leaned in for a kiss, and the baffling question of what on earth they'd been talking about for the last few minutes seemed suddenly unimportant. 'We'll eat, then?'

'Yeah. Is it okay for me to put my clothes on?'

She pursed her lips, as if thinking about the proposition. 'Just for a little while. I wouldn't want you to catch a chill.'

Waking up with Joe was lovely. This wasn't the first time she'd woken curled in his arms, but this time they couldn't love each other back to sleep again. She had to go to work.

Even so, the dash for the shower and a rushed breakfast was far more fun when Joe was around. And when Maisie phoned through the list of calls for the day, Neve didn't care how long it was, just that it meant that Joe would stay with her.

He wasn't like her ex-husband. Joe wasn't jealous or controlling and he didn't seem to feel the need to micromanage every part of her life. But, then, Matthew hadn't been like that when she'd first met him. Neve had often wondered how much of a part she'd played in the catastrophic change, which had turned the man she'd married into the man she'd divorced.

This time she had to do better. She'd married Matthew and then allowed him to walk all over her, submissive to his wants and needs. This time she'd be different. She'd make the ground rules clear from the very start and stick to them. She mustn't give Joe any reason to change.

But nothing could take the bright sheen off today. The feeling of being fully awake, having been half-asleep for such a long time. She and Joe worked doggedly together through her list of patients, and Neve left the tough questions until later.

'So we're done? Would you like to go and get something to eat?' They'd driven to all corners of Neve's allotted area so far today, and they were now on the south side, closest to the surgery and the town.

'I got a text from Maisie just now. Just one more to go.'

He nodded, keeping to himself whatever disappointment he felt at the thought of dinner being once more postponed. Another way that he wasn't like Matthew. Matthew would have phoned ahead, booked a table at the restaurant of his choice, and if anyone had upset his plans there would have been hell to pay.

Today was turning into a game of spot the difference. Neve hadn't given Matthew so much thought in months. She followed Joe to the car and consulted her phone, reading through the details of her next patient. 'Infected tattoo.'

'Where?'

'I don't know, Maisie didn't say. But apparently it's very swollen and beginning to suppurate.'

Joe rolled his eyes. 'I meant where's the house, not the tattoo. I'm the driver, remember?'

'Ah. Silly me.' She grinned up at him. It seemed that the separation of their roles was a joking matter now, instead of something to argue about. 'Only about two miles up the road. Here's the address.'

The snow had been melting all day, and driving conditions were getting easier. The two miles were accomplished with no delay and they drew up outside a large house, screened by trees and settled into the side of a hillside. Obviously newly built, it was a clever mix of local materials with modern design, the soaring glass windows framed with stone and the unusually angled roof clad with slate.

They stood for a while in the huge, glass-sided porch before the door was opened by a young man dressed only in pyjama bottoms, who looked as if he had just woken up.

'Dr Neve Harrison. I've come to see Andrew Martin.' Neve smiled at the youth, who seemed almost puzzled to find that someone was standing on the doorstep.

'Yeah. I'm Andrew.'

'Can we come in?' Joe stepped forward, and Andrew shrugged and nodded.

Andrew turned, and Neve caught her breath. On his shoulder blade was a large, swollen lump. At one time there might have been a design there, but that was now obscured by scabs and oozing sores. She flipped a glance at Joe, who took Andrew's arm, supporting him into the lounge.

It seemed a bit of a pity to sit him down on the plush leather sofa, but Joe didn't hesitate. Andrew slumped forward, his head resting on his knees, while Neve snapped on a pair of surgical gloves, handing another pair to Joe, who took them as automatically as they were offered but didn't put them on.

'What do you think?' As usual, he was standing back, not expressing any opinion of his own.

'Could be a reaction to the ink. It looks as if there's red and blue in there and they're the most likely colours to cause an allergic reaction. Or, more likely, it's infected.' She tapped the side of Andrew's face gently. 'Andrew... Andrew.'

'Yeah...'

'How long ago did you have this tattoo done?'

'Last week. Me and my mates went into town, and we all had one.'

'Is there anyone else here, Andrew?'

'Nah. My folks are away on holiday.'

Neve could smell stale alcohol on his breath. She mouthed to Joe to go and look in the kitchen and he nodded.

'Ow!' Andrew flinched when Neve gently touched the edge of the lump, to feel its consistency.

'Looks pretty painful.'

'Well, yeah.' Andrew's voice was heavily laced with sleepy sarcasm.

'Okay. Who called the surgery?' She couldn't imagine that Andrew had. He could hardly string a sentence together.

'My girlfriend. She's got a job in a bar. Had to go to work.'

Joe appeared in the doorway, and she met him there. 'The kitchen's full of beer bottles, pizza boxes and ashtrays. Smells like marijuana.'

'Right. Well, either he's got the mother of all hangovers, he's doped up to the eyeballs or he's got an infection.' Neve sighed. 'Probably all three. His skin feels warm to the touch.'

'Hospital?'

'Yes, we can't leave him here.' Neve pulled out her phone.

'We'll take him.'

'Is that okay? It'll probably be faster.' Neve had heard that the emergency services were still very stretched, and it was likely to be a long wait.

'Yeah. If he throws up on my back seat, I'll send his parents the cleaning bill.' Joe quirked his mouth downwards and strode towards Andrew. 'Come on, mate, wake up. We're going for a ride.'

Neve called Maisie and sent Joe to find some clothes for Andrew. The lad protested mightily when Neve tried to position a temporary dressing over the sore on his back, and Joe was suddenly there, grabbing his flailing arm and gently holding him still. Then Joe got him into his clothes, and together they supported Andrew into the car, Neve making him as comfortable as she could on the back seat, while Joe wound the seat belt around him.

'Okay?'

'Yeah. Let's go.' Neve settled into the seat next to Andrew, and Joe slid the car out of its parking spot and back onto the road.

Andrew had been seen almost immediately after Neve had briefed the triage nurse at the hospital. She found Joe in the A and E waiting room, reading a magazine about agricultural machinery, which someone had obviously left behind.

'What's the story?' He hadn't betrayed any clinical interest in the sore on Andrew's back when it had been right there in front of him, but it appeared that now was a good time to catch up on the details.

'They agree with me that it's an infection. They're keeping him in tonight because he's so out of it, and it looks as if he's developed a mild case of sepsis.'

Joe nodded. 'Good. Any news from Maisie?'

'Yeah, she's managed to contact Andrew's mother on a mobile number in the family's medical records. They'll drive back from London first thing in the morning.'

He put the magazine down on the chair next to him, stretching his arms. 'So are we done now?'

'Yes. Although would you mind if we popped in to the surgery? I could do with restocking my medical bag with a few things, and as we're so close...'

'No problem.' His mouth twitched into the smile that he'd given her last night. 'I can have a cup of tea with Maisie. Thank her for asking me to drive the most beautiful doctor in town.'

'You will not!'

She saw hurt in his eyes, but he covered it quickly with a grin. 'Ashamed of me?'

In her desperate attempts not to make any of the mistakes she'd made in the past she'd forgotten that Joe was vulnerable too. Neve stepped forward, between his outstretched legs, planting a kiss on his cheek. No one in the crowded waiting room looked round, they all had their own problems to think about. But the public acknowledgement was still thrilling.

'No. I just want you to be my little secret for a while…'

'*Little* secret?'

She leaned a little further forward, feeling his hands around her waist, supporting her weight. 'Great big beautiful secret,' she whispered in his ear, and he chuckled.

'Yeah. That's more like it.' He dropped a businesslike kiss on her cheek, and stood up. 'As we're in town, we could get something to eat and pick up some shopping if you like. The big stores are all open late this week.'

'Christmas shopping…?' Neve had hardly thought about when she was going to do the rest of her Christmas shopping. There was still another week to go, and she'd been so busy for the last couple of weeks.

'Most of my presents are already on their way to Canada, but I still need to pick up a few bits and pieces. How about you?'

Neve shrugged. 'I want to get a drill for my dad. Mum says his old one is making a funny noise.'

Joe grinned. 'Great. There's a DIY place not far from here. We could go there, if you want.'

'Just to have a look maybe. Not to buy.' It must have been apparent that many of the Christmas presents her family had received over the last few years had been chosen by Matthew, but her mum and dad had pretended not to notice. Neve had promised herself that this year she would choose her dad's present on her own, even if she knew nothing about power tools and was worried that she'd get the wrong thing.

'Sure. I'm always up for browsing around the DIY store.' He grinned at her. 'Particularly with you.'

Neve might as well have stayed in the car for all the notice that Matthew had ever taken of her when they'd been out shopping. But Joe seemed so different.

She should stop the comparisons, even if Joe did come off better every time. Joe was his own man, just as she wanted so badly to be her own woman. She'd fought so hard not to let Matthew define her, and she shouldn't let him define Joe either.

'The DIY store it is, then. I'll look at the drills, and you can look at everything else.'

CHAPTER TEN

FIRST THEY CALLED in at the surgery, and then went to the little Italian restaurant just around the corner for a hurried meal. Then they got down to the serious business of shopping, making for the glittering windows of one of the larger department stores.

'Right.' He stopped short inside the swing doors, apologising as someone elbowed him out of the way and rubbing his hands together as if this was a foray into the unknown. 'I know what I want to get.'

'That's a start…' Neve took the scrap of paper that he'd extracted from his wallet and focussed on the writing. A round, woman's hand. And this perfume was a classic.

'It's for Edie. I asked her daughter what I should get.'

'This is pretty expensive…'

He grinned. 'Yeah, that's what her daughter said. But I want to get Edie something nice, she's been very good to me. And she can't really afford this on her pension.'

Neve smiled up at him. 'You know what, you're a really nice guy.'

He gave her a look of mock horror. 'Be quiet! If Edie gets that idea into her head, I'll be done for. Do you know where the perfume is?'

Neve swept her gaze over the sea of heads, located the

perfume counter and beckoned for him to follow her. 'It should be somewhere here…'

While she methodically inspected each of the displays, Joe was picking up random tester bottles, sniffing tentatively at the tops.

'You have to spray it if you want to know what it's like.' She leaned towards him. Even with the heavy scent of cosmetics and perfume hanging in the air around them, she could discern his warm, clean smell. Like a creature sniffing out its mate.

'Think I'll pass on that.' He put the bottle down quickly.

'Not on yourself…' She sprayed a tester strip, waving it under his nose.

'Ugh! That's horrible!' He grabbed another bottle at random, spraying it onto a second strip.

The scent's strong statement hit her like a punch in the face. She'd never liked it, but it was Matthew's favourite. And the most shaming part of it all was that Neve had let him dictate that she wear it all the time.

'Hmm…' He shrugged, discarding the bottle, and a sudden calculating glint showed in his eyes. 'So which one do *you* like? What do you wear when you're off duty?'

'The same as when I'm on duty. Nothing.' Neve was done with having anyone else buy personal things for her. Clothes, shoes, perfume. That was her territory now.

'Ah.' He bent towards her, and she felt the scrape of his stubble against her neck. 'That's why you always smell so gorgeous.'

'Stop it.' She loved it, but Christmas shopping was serious business. 'Focus, will you?'

'Right.' He scanned the length of the display in front of them. 'Is that it?'

An assistant appeared out of nowhere, flashing Joe a glittering smile. 'These, sir?' She spread manicured fingers over the range, from relatively inexpensive to don't-even-think-about-it.

'How about that one?' Joe pointed to a generously sized bottle, somewhere in the middle, and turned to Neve. 'I don't want to embarrass her…'

'I think it's a lovely present. Although I imagine that Edie will tell you that you've got the wrong thing.'

''Course she will. That's half the fun.' He turned to the assistant, pulling his wallet out of his pocket.

'Gift-wrapped, sir?'

'No, thanks. I want to wrap it myself.'

The assistant threw him a more spontaneous smile. 'Would you like one of these?' She reached under the counter and drew out a small tester pack, prettily packaged and containing tiny amounts of six different perfumes.

'Oh. Thanks very much.' Joe took the pack, stared at it, and handed it awkwardly over to Neve. 'That's probably more your department.'

She took the pack and stowed it in her handbag. 'Thanks.'

He nodded, and turned his attention back to the assistant, handing her his bank card. Neve curled her fingers around the packet in her bag. The scents looked nice, and she might just try one of them. But it would be *her* choice when she did.

Joe brightened considerably once paper and ribbon had been chosen and they were heading for the DIY store. He seemed to have the geography of the large tin shed well fixed in his mind, and Neve followed him past seemingly endless shelves of paint and tools until they got to a small enclosure, where an assistant guarded the power tools.

'You're looking for something, sir?' The assistant approached Joe.

'Not me. The lady's looking for a drill.'

'Ah.' The assistant glanced at her and walked over to the smallest drill in the display. 'Something like this, perhaps?'

Joe didn't look very impressed. 'What about this one?' He ran his finger along a large, complicated-looking model.

'Very heavy for a woman.' The assistant was still speaking to Joe, as if Neve didn't exist.

Joe seemed to have already dismissed the man's advice and didn't bother to explain. 'Well, perhaps we'll try a couple out and get back to you.'

With that Joe turned to Neve, beckoning her over to where he was standing. 'What do you think?'

'I don't know, really. Which one do you think's best?' She could hear his opinion at least.

Joe puffed out a breath, as if the question was a hard one. 'It depends on what kind of work your dad wants to do.'

'Nothing in particular. Drilling holes in the wall to hang pictures. He built a garden shed once.'

'Well, these are two good general-purpose ones. Do you want to pick them up, see how they feel?'

The question threw Neve completely for a moment. *She* should see how they felt?

'Yes… Yeah, I do.'

Joe grinned, signalling to the assistant to unlock the demonstration models. Then he dismissed the man again, and put one of the drills into Neve's hands.

'How am I meant to hold it?'

'Put your finger on the trigger… No, you'll need to be able to reach the trigger lock as well. Like this…'

Suddenly he was at her back, his arms stretching around her, his hands over hers, holding the drill. Instinctively she moved in closer.

'That's it. How does that feel?'

It felt great. His arms around her. His taut, unyielding body at her back.

'Lovely.'

'The drill.' She could feel his breath on the back of her neck. 'Focus…'

'Oh. Yes. I don't really have anything to compare it with.'

'All right, try the other one.' Joe reached for the second drill, putting it into her hands.

'Oh, this is better. More balanced.'

Joe nodded. 'Right, well, there are a few other considerations.'

Corded or cordless, what kinds of bits to buy, power rating, speeds, gears, torque. There was much more to it all than Neve had suspected, and Joe seemed to have a handle on it all.

'So, which one do you think?'

He couldn't have said a nicer thing if he'd tried. But even though Joe had given her all the information, she was still undecided. 'Do you mind if I just look at them all again quickly?'

'Take your time. I'll be over there.' He pointed to a display of unlikely-looking tools, which Neve couldn't fathom the use of.

She made her choice, sorted through the boxes to find one that wasn't crushed or dented, and found Joe immersed in conversation with another man who was browsing the shelves.

'Decided?'

'Yes. What do you think of this one?'

Joe gave the box she was carrying a glance. 'I think he'll really like it.'

It was late when Neve carried her precious parcel out of the DIY store. Joe had automatically reached for it, the way he always did when there was anything to carry, and had grinned when she'd snatched it from him. This she was carrying herself.

They didn't discuss where they were going, just drove. Out of the lights of the city, plunging into the darkness of the country lanes, where only the car's headlights illuminated their path. When Neve had first come here, the darkness on roads without streetlights had been intimidating. Now it was the bright lights of the city that seemed wrong, polluting the atmosphere and blocking the soft glow of the stars on a clear night.

The car began to shudder, and Joe cursed under his breath, easing his foot off on the accelerator and bringing the vehicle to a gentle halt.

'What's the matter?'

'It feels like a puncture. Stay there, I'll go and see.'

'Okay.'

The rosy glow retreated a little and Neve got out of the car. 'Do you have—?'

She slipped forward and suddenly she was falling into the darkness. Cushioned by her bulky clothes and the deep snow, she rolled down the bank beside the road. She was vaguely aware of Joe's shout, and then she hit the bottom.

She lifted her head, and there was Joe, at the top of the bank, a dark shadow behind a torch beam, which urgently swept the bank, before coming to rest on her.

'You okay?'

'Yes, I'm all right. The snow broke my fall.' She struggled to her feet and then slipped over again and decided to stay put until Joe had found something else to do other than stare at her.

'I said to stay there.' His voice was edged with frustration.

'I heard you. I'm not in the habit of obeying instructions without question.' She folded her arms across her chest defiantly.

'So I've noticed. Are you going to get up?' He had the demeanour of someone who could wait.

'Not just yet.'

'You'll get soaked.'

'That's why I'm wearing waterproofs. So I don't get wet.'

Suddenly he moved, sliding sideways down the bank, the arc of powdered snow that flew from his boots glistening in the waving torchlight and spraying her jacket. He was still on his feet when he reached the bottom.

'Stop showing off.'

'Then get up.' He grinned, holding up a handful of snow and training the torch onto it, just in case she'd missed his intention. 'Or else…'

There was only one possible answer to that. 'Or else what?' Neve flopped back into the snow. 'I thought you had a tyre to change.'

'I thought you were going to stay in the car.' He planted his feet on either side of her hips then dropped to his knees, brandishing the snowball.

'Don't you dare, Joe.'

Too late. His eyes, the curve of his lips dared everything. And she dared him right back, her body melting, ready to be moulded into whatever shape he wanted.

He ditched the snowball, pinning her arms down over her head. 'You think I don't dare?'

'I think you *do* dare.'

So did she.

He bent, kissing her. She'd been missing that kiss all day. Not the brief brush of his lips against hers but a searching, demanding onslaught that melted the last remains of her resistance. His gloved hand slid across the outside of her waterproofs, finding the exact place where her breast was under layers of clothing.

The torch had gone out and they were in complete darkness. She felt his hand pulling her knees apart, and then his body settling onto hers.

'You can't. Not in this temperature.'

His chuckle sounded in her ear and his stubble scraped her cheek. 'I like a woman who knows the limits of human physiology.' His body began to move against hers, a delicious friction that could only arouse, not satisfy. 'What about the limits of human imagination…?'

She was there already, her body trembling for his touch. Neve groaned with frustration.

'So you'll help me change the tyre, then? Hold the torch steady and hand me the lug wrench when I ask for it?'

'Yeah.' Anything…

'And you'll come back to my place tonight?'

She hadn't intended to. He seemed to sense her hesitation and his hand slid to the back of her leg, pulling it up and around his hips. 'I'll make it worth your while.'

'I know.' She felt a tiny, cold trickle at the back of her shoulder and shuddered. 'By the way, I think the high-performance waterproofing's just stopped performing.'

He was standing over her almost before she could even register that he was gone, pulling her to her feet and brushing the snow off her back. 'Are you okay?'

Stupid question. 'Fine. Hurry up with that tyre.'

CHAPTER ELEVEN

THE THAW WAS well under way now. When Neve woke the following morning the snow in Leminster High Street, outside Joe's window, was almost gone. And even when they drove out into the countryside the roads were clear, the snowploughs and the warmer weather having done their job.

They were finished by five in the evening, and this time Neve was less of a walkover. Tomorrow was Saturday and she had the weekend off. She told Joe that she needed some sleep and he made no comment, other than quirking his lips down in an expression of disappointment.

'You fancy the movies tomorrow afternoon, then? Is there anything you want to see?' He seemed unwilling to leave until he had a firm date fixed for when he'd see her again.

'Yes, a couple of films. Why don't you come round for lunch?'

The familiar ritual of getting out of the car and letting Joe carry her bags to the door followed, then a kiss, light on her lips, as if anything more would be too much of a temptation.

'Goodnight, honey.'

They'd been together now, non-stop, for more than sixty hours. Almost enough time to work a virus out of your system, but Joe was more tenacious than that and she wasn't even beginning to work up a resistance to him. Leaving him was more difficult than she'd thought.

'Goodnight, Joe.' She'd see him tomorrow. And tonight she would get some sleep.

The house was clean, a bunch of flowers stood on the kitchen table, and the potatoes were peeled and ready in a pan on the stove. Neve had woken at her usual time that morning, had got out of bed and been unable to linger over breakfast. At some point she'd probably sleep for twelve hours straight, but right now she felt more awake than she'd been for months. Years.

At twelve sharp she heard the doorbell. Dropped the knife that she had just used to skin two large onions and ran to the door.

'Hey, there.' He grinned.

She'd missed that smile. Missed his warm body next to her in the bed, which was far too cold to sleep in without him. The sofa bed in the kitchen, which had seemed so cosy before, now felt deeply unsatisfactory.

'Hi.' She stood back from the door and he bent to pick up the post from the mat, handing it to her before he tramped through to the kitchen. No kiss.

He remedied that as soon as she'd put the bundle of letters down on the table, catching her in his arms and moulding her against him. 'I missed you last night.'

'Yeah? I would have thought you'd be sleeping like a baby...'

'Nope. I was thinking of you.' He was clean-shaven this morning, his cheek smooth against hers, still cold from the air outside.

'What were you thinking?'

He kissed her. Yeah, she'd been thinking that too...

'I was wondering what you were going to make me for lunch today.'

'Oh, really?'

'It's important.'

She unclasped his hands from behind her, walking to the stove and picking up the frying pan. 'Bangers and mash.'

'Nice. Local sausages?'

'Of course. From the farmers' market.'

Joe grinned. 'You really are my kind of woman.'

Neve laughed. 'And you really are easy, aren't you.'

'Me?' He put his hand on his chest with an expression of disbelief. 'I'll have you know that I'm not even slightly easy. Are you making onion gravy?'

'I thought you might take charge of that.' Neve walked to the table, sorting through her letters. A couple of bills, which she put to one side for later, and a bunch of coloured envelopes.

'Why don't you open them?' He nodded towards the mantelpiece, which was already two deep in Christmas cards. 'I think you've got about a square inch of spare space up there.'

She grinned and started tearing the envelopes open. 'Ah. That's nice.' A shower of glitter fell from the front of the card and she brushed it off the table. 'Auntie Maureen.' She showed him the inside of the card.

He nodded in approval, taking the card and looking at the snow scene on the front. 'Have you got a tree?'

'Not yet. I've been too busy.'

'You want me to pick one up for you? I could go on Monday, if you're not going to need me to drive you.'

'I don't think I will. We're planning to resume the normal rota on Monday so I'll be over at the surgery. And I thought I might give a tree a miss this year as I'm going back to London for Christmas.'

'That's only for a couple of days, though. Christmas lasts longer than that.'

Christmas seemed to have already started, and would probably last right through till March at this rate. 'Okay, then. If it's no trouble, thanks.'

Neve tore open the last of the envelopes. A thick, heavy card, which looked like something that a company would send, well designed, tasteful and completely lacking in any sparkle. When she flipped it open she felt the smile slide from her face and crash to the floor.

Happy Christmas.
    I saw you on TV the other day, and realised that I love you more than ever.
    Let's talk in the New Year.
Matthew

Matthew's precise, rather too artful script, with a flourish at the end of his name and two kisses. Neve closed the card and then decided she didn't want it anywhere near her. Or Joe. As casually as she could she tore it into two, walking over to the kitchen waste bin and dropping it inside. Then, for good measure, she threw the onion skins from the chopping board on top of it.

'I'd better start on lunch if we're going to get to the pictures in time.'

He didn't reply, and when Neve turned to look at Joe his eyes were thoughtful. She almost wanted him to ask, but perhaps he didn't want to know. She turned back to the onions, slicing them into halves.

He was quiet on his feet when he wanted to be. She didn't hear him cross the room and Neve started when he wound his arms around her waist from behind. 'Anything you want to talk about?' He brushed a kiss against the back of her head.

'Not really.'

He took the knife out of her hand and put it down on the chopping board, turning her round to face him. 'And I suppose that's just the onions…' His finger brushed at her cheek.

'Actually, it is.' The card from Matthew had surprised and unsettled her. Nothing more. She had no tears for him, and no love left either. If he got in touch with her again, she'd tell him so.

'Then you won't mind telling me who the card was from.'

That was different. How Joe might feel about the card *was* important. But Neve couldn't lie to him.

'It was from my ex-husband. I didn't even know he had my address.'

'You didn't tell him where you are?'

'When I left London I wanted to leave my marriage behind. It wasn't as if I was talking to him about anything else.' Neve heaved a sigh. 'He saw me on TV doing that stupid interview, and I suppose it's not too difficult to find someone once you know their general whereabouts.'

He nodded, his face grave. 'He hurt you that much?'

'It's history, Joe.'

'Yeah. But sometimes the past leaves scars…'

'Yes.' Her fingers found his lips, trying to brush the words away. 'I'm sorry, Joe.'

'Don't be. It was just something that happened.' His face softened again. 'Sometimes I wake in the night and it's as if I'm right back there.'

Neve caught her breath. 'You said you didn't remember…'

He shook his head, as if that was a minor detail. 'What I'm saying is that when you're hurt, physically or emotionally, the shock of it stays with you. You think you've healed, you may look as if you've healed, but it takes a while before your emotions catch up with that fact.'

She hugged him tight. There weren't any words. None that made much sense anyway. She felt his chest heave as he took a breath.

'Don't you think it's time to talk about it?'

Joe had watched Neve tentatively taking hold of this new relationship, acting sometimes as if it might burn her. He knew that she'd been hurt and that at some point it was all going to come to a head. It seemed that now was that point.

'What do you say I make a cup of tea?' There was something to be said for Edie's obsession with the perfect cup of tea—it served to lessen the tension a little. And while he was busying himself, it seemed to give Neve some time to think. As soon as he sat down she started to talk.

'I married Matthew when I was twenty-three, not even out of medical school. He was intelligent and charming. He'd made a lot of money in property when he was very young, and he wanted to give me everything.'

'Sounds like a good start.' Joe reached for the teapot and began to pour the tea.

'Yeah, I thought so too. Then the moods started. This little thing wasn't right or I hadn't looked smart enough for his friends. He was working pretty hard and I thought that he was just under stress.'

Alarm bells started to ring at the back of Joe's head. He ignored them and nodded her on.

'Before long he was dictating practically everything. Where we lived, who we saw, what kinds of things I wore. My perfume…' The words seemed to stick in her throat.

'And so you left him.' Joe reckoned that was a pretty safe assumption.

'No. I should have done, I know, but I wanted my marriage to work. I thought it was my fault. Can you understand that?'

'No.'

She flushed suddenly, bright red, tears forming in her eyes. Then came the anger. Anger seemed to be Neve's answer to everything that touched her personally, and Joe imagined it was what had got her through. It drove her to her feet, her face distorted. 'Then you should go.'

'Wait. Hold up there…' Joe was on his feet too. 'Will you just sit down? Please.'

'You either get it or you don't, Joe. I can't explain…' Neve sat back down with a bump, glaring at him.

'What I don't understand is why a guy would want to change anything about you.'

'Stop being nice.'

'And stop being so damn angry, Neve. You're an intelligent, capable woman and you push me away because of what another guy's done.'

'I know. I'm sorry.' She stared at him, one lonely tear tricking down the side of her face.

'What? What is it, Neve?' The suspicion of something dark throbbed insistently in his head, making him feel sick to his stomach. 'Did he ever hurt you?'

'He…' The dark red flush of her cheeks was like his own scars, a badge of shame at having been hurt.

'Okay.' He reached across the table, his hands trembling as he took hers. 'You took me as I am. We can do this together.'

He steadied his gaze on hers. Somewhere, deep in her eyes, he found the strength to stay calm and just listen to what she had to say.

She took a deep breath. 'I was pregnant. We didn't plan it, but I was so happy. I thought Matt would be too, but he said it wasn't the right time. He reckoned it was best for me to leave it a few years, get more established with my career, and then…then *he'd* think about it. I didn't see it at the time but he was just terrified that someone else might take his place. That he wouldn't be my top priority any more.'

Joe's felt his lip curl. 'His loss. His weakness…'

'My weakness, too. I knew in my heart that our home wasn't the place to bring up a child but I tried to persuade Matt. We argued about it for weeks, and it was the one thing I never backed down on. Then one night I told him I was leaving. He punched me in the face.'

Rage. All Joe could think about was finding this guy and… But punching the walls because he couldn't get his hands on the brute who had hurt her was the last thing that Neve needed from him right now. Slowly he reached out, brushing the side of her face. 'What happened then?'

'I ran. He was very angry and he grabbed hold of me but I managed to get away from him. I got into my car and drove away… I shouldn't have been driving, one of my eyes was beginning to swell, but…'

'You were protecting your child.'

'It seemed like that at the time. I was turning into my parents' road when a kid on a motorcycle shot out in front of me out of nowhere. I swerved to avoid him and went into someone's front wall.'

'You were hurt?'

'I wasn't going very fast and the airbag saved me from anything but a jolt. But my face was bleeding and someone called an ambulance and they took me to hospital. My mum told them I was pregnant and they checked me out and said everything was fine…but two days later I lost my baby.'

Joe had already guessed that she must have lost the baby. But still there were no words.

'I'm so sorry.'

'Thank you.' She gave a trembling smile and Joe almost

choked with emotion. 'When Matthew came to see me and said it was all for the best, that we could put everything behind us and start again, I threw him out. After that, my dad wouldn't let him into the house.'

'I'm glad your parents were there to support you.'

She pressed her lips together. 'I should take my share of the blame, too.'

How did she work that one out? 'You know, don't you, that it's unlikely the car accident caused your miscarriage. In the first trimester the baby's very well protected...'

'That's not the point, Joe. If I'd left when I first knew I was pregnant, there's a chance...' She shook her head.

'You can go around in circles like that for ever, Neve.' In his moment of greatest need Joe found himself clinging to the training he'd been given, the profession that he had promised he would never again practise. 'As a doctor, I could tell you all the statistics, all the probabilities. You know them as well as I do.'

She looked at him steadily. 'I thought you didn't admit to being a doctor any more.'

'Some things are more important than the rules you make for yourself. I won't let you believe that this was your fault.'

'How can you really know?'

'Because I know you, Neve. I know that you were thinking always of your child and that you did everything you could.'

'I can't forget, though...'

'Nor should you, ever. But grieving is a process. It's a way of making peace with the past so that you can move forward.'

Her gaze searched his face, as if looking for clues. Joe didn't have any. All he could do was be there for her.

'You know the two things I've always wanted were

to be, a doctor and to be a mother...' She gave him a teary smile.

'Not a wife?' Joe wouldn't much blame her, after what she'd been through.

'Yeah, a wife too, one day. I didn't want to mention that in case I frightened you off.' She gave a little laughing shrug, and suddenly the tension in the room broke.

'You don't frighten me...' The thought of hurting her suddenly terrified Joe.

She chuckled. 'I know. That's one of the things I like about you.'

'Well, I think you'd be a great mother. I already know you're a great doctor.' Joe's heart began to thump in his chest. If the lesson from Neve's past told her that she'd married the wrong man, that she should move on and find someone who could be a good father to her children, the lesson from his told him that he wasn't that guy. He wasn't someone who could be trusted with the welfare of others.

But the hope on her face was so precious to him. He should concentrate on that and not his own doubts.

'Thank you. I really appreciate what you've said.'

'I just told you what I see.'

She rose from her chair and perched on his lap. Joe pulled her in close, allowing the happiness of having her in his arms block out everything else.

'You want to risk some lunch, then? Since I don't frighten you...' She smiled up at him.

'Yeah. Let's take a chance on it.'

CHAPTER TWELVE

THE HOURS HAD slid by, like honey on his tongue. Lunch, and then the drive into town for the cinema. But in the darkness of the auditorium it was impossible to keep himself from his thoughts any more. By the time the lights came back up he'd lost the plot of the movie but the scenario that had projected itself in his head was entirely clear to him.

'You're very quiet.' She nudged him gently in the ribs as they walked along the lane to her front gate. 'Didn't you like the film?'

'No, it was fine…' Joe had no feelings one way or the other about it.

'I thought the part about waiting for the information to download from the laptop was a bit much. If the guy had just tucked it under his arm and run off with it, he'd have been free and clear before the guards arrived.'

Joe felt himself smile, almost against his will. Neve obviously hadn't liked the film any more than the other movie-goers he'd heard talking about it on the way out. But she didn't let the little things in life get her down, she just smiled about them. He felt an overwhelming urge—no, a duty—not to quash that irrepressible optimism.

'I guess they had to get the chase over the rooftops in

somehow.' That was about the only part of the movie he remembered.

'No, you must have nodded off, that was later.' She took out her keys, letting them both into the house, and Joe followed her into the kitchen. 'Mind you, that chase over the roof was another thing. He'd have broken a leg, landing on the pavement after that fall, not just got up and run away...'

She stopped talking and looked up at him. He saw the concern grow in her face, the unmistakeable flash in her eyes that signalled she knew that something was wrong. 'Why don't you take your coat off, Joe?'

'I'm...not staying.' He had to be careful what he said. Neve was vulnerable, and he shouldn't make this all about her. It wasn't, it was all about him.

'That's okay.' Her mouth twitched downwards. 'You can have a cup of tea, though, can't you?'

The urge to say yes, to allow the evening to drift gently to a point where he would take her to bed and hold her for the last time, was almost irresistible. But Joe knew how to resist the irresistible. And however many other faults he might have, he'd never acted dishonestly just to slake his own libido.

'No. Neve, I think that we should take a break.'

Her hands clenched tightly together, making a small wringing motion. He could almost see the cogs whirring in her head. Dammit, she was doing just what he didn't want her to do and blaming herself.

'That's...that's okay. Whatever you want, Joe.'

'It's not what I want. But I haven't been quite honest with you.'

She sat down at the kitchen table with a bump. 'There's nothing that you can say that I won't listen to...'

He knew that. But it was complicated, and now wasn't the time to burden her with it. 'I'm going back to Canada. In a couple of weeks' time.' The move came as news to him, as well as being an obvious shock to her. But the lease on his cottage was up in the new year, and he could pack up and move in a couple of days.

'I don't believe you.' She jutted her chin at him determinedly.

'I know I should have told you…'

'I don't believe you, Joe. I just don't believe that you'd sleep with me without telling me that.'

It was almost a compliment. It would have been unthinkable to Joe as well, and the fact that she knew that warmed him, when he shouldn't really have been taking any comfort from any of this.

'Neve, I—'

'Take your coat off.' A tear rolled down her cheek.

He couldn't deny her that one thing. He threw his jacket across the back of a chair and sat down opposite her. 'Neve, I am going to go back home. I've been thinking about things and…' Only the truth was going to do. A watered-down version, at least.

'When you told me about your marriage I was furious with the guy who hurt you. And then, when I thought about it, I realised that I'm no better than he is. I don't want to see you hurt again, you don't deserve that.'

'Then don't do it.'

'That's exactly why I'm doing this.' She'd played right into his hands but it gave Joe no pleasure. 'I can't give you the things you want and it would be dishonest of me to string you along.'

'Is that a way of telling me that you changed your mind?'

'No. It's a way of telling you that I can't give you what you want. A lot happened to me when I was in the army, and I'm still struggling with that. I don't want to…I *can't* take responsibility for other lives any more.'

'You don't have to take responsibility for me.' She

seemed to stiffen, starting to withdraw from him. It was the beginning of the end, and now Joe just wanted to get things over quickly.

'Look, I know that this is something that's way in the future. But one day, if things work out between us, it's natural to want to settle down and have children. I can't do that and I don't think I'll ever be able to. It just isn't in me any more.'

'I haven't asked you for that, Joe. We've known each other…what…two weeks. Less than that…' He could see in her eyes that she'd thought about it. He'd thought about it too. The connection between them was too strong not to have wondered if it might last a lifetime.

'I know. But if two weeks turned into two years, then my answer would still be the same. Then I'd be the guy who strung you along, who never told you. So I'm telling you now.'

She looked at him blankly. She knew as well as he did now that this wasn't going to work.

'You deserve—you need—someone who wants the same things as you, Neve.'

Anger flared in her eyes. The final denial of how much this hurt. 'Don't be so bloody arrogant. Who are you to tell me what I need?'

The man who loves you. The man who's going to leave you. Joe reached for his coat.

'If you go now, you don't come back.' She flung the words at him. That was okay. Joe knew that this was his fault already. He stood, hurrying for the front door before his courage failed him, half expecting, half wanting her to follow. She didn't. He closed the door behind him, got into his car, and drove away.

Thinking about it was useless. Something had happened to Joe, something he wouldn't talk about, and Neve couldn't work out what it was. She'd looked up PTSD in her medical books and on the internet, dwelling on the parts that mentioned feelings of guilt and inability to commit. But that wasn't the whole story. And he had it right in one respect. If their relationship had survived, if they'd got married, then Neve would have wanted children. If Joe hadn't, it might well have been a breaking point.

She'd feel better about this once she got it into perspective. She'd known Joe for a total of two weeks, then he'd made it clear that he didn't want to take things any further. It really didn't qualify as the romance of the century, and mooning around as if it was was plain stupid. Three days at home with her family, over Christmas, would stop her from thinking about him for every waking moment and dreaming about him when she finally succumbed to sleep.

The week dragged by in a numb succession of coughs, colds and sprains, and finally it was Friday morning, Christmas Eve. Neve was up early to finish her packing, ready to catch the train down to London at midday. The bedroom was cold, and when Neve opened the curtains to peer outside, she realised why. From the look of the lane outside, it had been snowing all night.

'Damn!' Possibly not the most festive of reactions, but she had to travel today. Grabbing her laptop, she got back under the bedclothes and searched for updates on whether the trains were running.

It was the first thing in days that made her feel even remotely like smiling. Trains to London were on time and, despite adverse weather conditions, no delays were expected for intercity services. She might have to walk to the station but she'd get there. Neve snapped her laptop shut with a grin, put a thick cardigan on over her pyjamas, and hurried down to the kitchen to brew some coffee.

Two hours later she was ready to go, with an hour and

a half before her train left. Before she put three hundred miles between her and Joe.

Her phone rang. Despite herself, Neve's first thought was that he'd called to wish her a happy Christmas.

Clearly not. Neve shook her head and swiped her thumb across the screen.

'Hi, Maisie. How's the mulled wine going?' Neve had shared her recipe with Maisie the previous day.

'Neve. I'm sorry to do this to you…'

Neve resisted the temptation to throw the phone out of the window. 'What is it?'

'Emma called. She's on her way back here for Christmas, and the train she's on has broken down in the tunnel, just before you get to Leminster.'

'Yes, I know where you mean…' Neve wasn't quite sure what she could do about Maisie's daughter being stuck on a train.

'Apparently they waited an hour and a maintenance crew arrived. The driver got off the train with them and started shovelling snow or something, and then he collapsed. They got him back onto the train and Em's doing her best—there's no phone reception in the tunnel but she's passing messages back to one of the crew, who talked to Ted. He says it sounds like a mild heart attack.'

'All right. I'm on my way, Maisie. Let Emma know if you can. Have you called the emergency services?'

'Yes. Ted's on his way too, but he just phoned and said that the snow's pretty deep and it's slow going.'

'Yeah, I reckon I'll have to walk it but it's not far. I can get there much quicker than either Ted or the ambulance. Tell him to come back home and I'll call and let you both know what's going on.'

'Thanks, Neve. Would it help if I called Joe?'

She didn't want to see Joe. She didn't need him, she

could handle this on her own. 'It's okay. There's no way
he can get through any quicker than I can.'

'Okay. Well, let me know if there's anything you need.'

'Will do. Thanks for calling, Maisie.'

A short, strained laugh. 'You don't mean that.'

'Yes and no. I wouldn't have forgiven you if you hadn't.'

Neve ended the call, and sat motionless, looking at her
phone for a moment. She had no idea of the situation on
that train. And yet she'd just made a judgement call.

It was a bit rich, calling it a judgement call. There wasn't
much professional judgement involved, more personal
hubris. She sighed, running her finger down her contacts
list. Joe answered on the second ring.

'Neve… Hi.'

His voice sounded relaxed, pleased she'd called. How
could he have forgotten so soon that they were supposed
to have just broken each other's hearts?

'Joe, there's a train stranded in the tunnel just out of
Leminster. There may be a casualty…'

'You need me to drive you?'

'No. The quickest way from here is to walk across the
fields. I may need some medical assistance, though, and
you're the only other doctor in the immediate area.'

There was a pause. 'Neve, I don't think that's appropriate.'

Anger flared. She'd just put her pride aside and called
him, and he'd turned her down flat. Fine. She could manage without him. In fact, she could probably manage a
great deal better without him. 'Okay. Whatever you say.'

She ended the call, without waiting for his reply. If Joe
said he wasn't coming, she had no time to mess around
talking to him. She had to hurry.

Quickly she packed the things she might need into one
bag and pulled her coat and boots on. Her luggage, one
small case with her clothes in it and a larger one full of

presents stood ready behind the front door, and she pushed them ruefully to one side. Christmas was going to have to wait.

It was still snowing, and it was hard going down to the end of the lane. But the road beyond was relatively clear. Neve took a moment to look to her left, in the direction of the station, and then turned right. Two hundred yards further on there was a footpath, which skirted the fields and then ran parallel to the railway line.

It took ten minutes on a good day to get from here to the tunnel. But today, with a heavy bag to carry, and in the deep snow, she'd be lucky to make it in twenty. She put her head down and started to walk.

She would have seen the figure walking towards her across the fields sooner if she'd not been concentrating on each step she took. Trying not to slip on the uneven ground. Trying to walk as fast as she could. When she did look up, it was within shouting distance.

Joe. His hood almost covered his face, but his bulk, the grace with which he strode through the deep snow were unmistakeable. Neve cursed herself roundly for the moment of sheer happiness that forced itself on her before she had time to think.

'I thought you weren't coming,' she shouted to him—*at* him—as the gap closed between them.

'I changed my mind.'

He must have changed it pretty quickly. Even at the punishing pace he was keeping up, it would have taken him at least as long as it had her to get to this point. 'Right…' Neve was too out of breath for argument.

'Let me take that.' He fell into step beside her.

'I can manage.'

'Give me the bag.' There was a glint of no-nonsense steel about him. The same set determination that she'd seen on Holcombe Crag where practicality, not etiquette, was the order of the day. Neve pulled the strap of her bag over her head and gave it to him.

'Thank you.' He hooked the strap over his shoulder.

What for? She was just getting the job done, in the best way she knew how. They'd make better time this way, and that was all that mattered.

'Why are you here, Joe?' She didn't stop walking.

'You asked me to come.'

'Yeah, and you said that it was inappropriate. You've decided to come and watch?'

'No, I decided it was inappropriate of me to not to offer help in this situation.' He seemed as intent as she was in keeping this on a purely professional basis. He wasn't there for her. He was there for the people on that train.

'Your experience?' Irrational disappointment lend harshness to her words.

'Military general surgeon. I also have experience of combat casualty care.'

Neve nodded. Joe had better experience of dealing with the kind of situation that might be waiting for them than she did. Whether he had the heart to use that experience remained to be seen.

CHAPTER THIRTEEN

SHE NEEDED TO start working with him, not against him. If Neve wanted Joe to come through for her, she needed to give him a bit of support and stop treating him like the guy who'd broken her heart six days ago. Even if he was.

'The situation is that there's a man on the train who may have had a mild heart attack. There may be other injuries that I'm not aware of.'

'We'll find out soon enough.' Up ahead the line disappeared into a tunnel, banked with snow. 'I think I see the back of the train.'

It was snowing heavily now, and visibility was limited, but there was a bright flash of colour at the mouth of the tunnel. As Neve watched, a figure in high-visibility gear detached itself from the opening, waving at them.

The ground sloped down towards the railway line and there was a line of bushes curtaining a chain-link fence and barring their way. Joe began to slide carefully down the slope, and Neve followed him.

'Careful…these have thorns…' The bushes were designed to keep people out, forming a deep, prickly, hedge. Joe started to break a path through them, holding the spiny branches to one side so she could get through.

'We're going to need to climb— Ow!' Neve caught her sleeve on a thorn, and Joe turned to unhook her.

'One thing at a time.' He broke his way through to the fence, just as the man in the high-vis suit reached the other side. 'Dr Neve Harrison and Dr Joe Lamont.'

It was the first time she'd heard him say it, and there was no time to even think about what it meant. Joe pulled a small pack from his back and unzipped it.

'We didn't know which way you'd be coming. I'll have to go back down and get some wire cutters.' The man turned and started to pick his way back down the embankment.

'Yeah, right. We'll wait.' Joe's tone was heavy with sarcasm as he drew a pair of wire cutters from his pack.

'Does this count as vandalism of railway property?' Neve murmured the words to him.

'Guess I'll find that out later. If anyone asks, I forced you into it.' The ghost of a smile tugged at his mouth and then he turned, snipping at the links of the fence.

'I should be doing that.' The man toiled back up towards them again.

'Sorry.' Joe slipped the cutters into the pack and held the gap in the fence open for Neve to step through. 'It's already done.'

Neve suppressed a smile. When she was through to the other side, Joe handed her the bags and followed her.

'You'll have to follow my instructions. Health and safety rules…' The man seemed intent on emphasising that he was in charge here.

'Fine.' Joe started to stride on ahead. 'And you'll have to keep up.'

Neve slithered down the steep incline of the embankment behind Joe, almost losing her footing. But Joe was there, one arm held out towards her to steady her.

'Keep away from the rails. Don't touch anything.' Joe's advice seemed the most reliable and Neve nodded. 'Here. Just slide down this last bit and I'll catch you.'

Neve tried to keep her balance so that Joe wouldn't have to grab hold of her, but she couldn't. She skated down the last couple of feet of the embankment, right into his arms.

No eye contact. Joe seemed suddenly to be looking one way and Neve the other. He set her unceremoniously back onto her feet, turning towards the mouth of the tunnel.

'I've got to stay here with the phone.' The railway guy was breathing heavily from the effort of keeping up with them. 'Adam Grimshaw's my boss, he's the one you need to speak to.'

'Okay, thanks. Up here?' Joe pointed to a steep gangway that had been lashed together to give access to the last door of the back carriage.

'Yep. Want a hand?'

'No, thanks, we're good.' Joe climbed up to the open door, depositing the bags inside, and reached down towards Neve, wrapping his hand around her arm. Her boots slid on the gangway, but he steadied her and pulled her up into the train.

It was dark inside the carriage. Joe bent to open his pack and withdrew a couple of torches, handing one to her. When he switched his on, playing it around the carriage, Neve could see another railway employee hurrying towards them, one hand raised to shade his eyes from the torchlight.

'You're the doctor?'

'Drs Harrison and Lamont. We've been told to ask for Adam Grimshaw.' Neve stepped forward.

'That's me. I'm co-ordinating things here until we can get everyone off the train. Thanks for getting here so quickly. The driver's ill and there's a woman been injured as well.'

Two casualties. Neve turned to Joe. 'I'll take the heart attack, you have a look at the other injury.'

He nodded, his face tightening into a mask. 'Right you are.'

Whatever his reservations, it seemed that Joe was going to do it. That was all she needed to know.

The man led them through the connecting doors to the next carriage. Groups of people sat in the darkness, and every face turned towards them, pale in the torchlight, as they hurried down the centre aisle.

'All right, folks. Stay in your seats, please. Doctor coming through.' Adam's voice rose above the hubbub of murmured questions.

The next carriage was full of people. The same pale faces, the same questions, only this time the sound of a young child crying sliced through the air. Neve made a mental note that as soon as the emergency cases had been seen, she'd find the mother and make sure that both were all right.

'We got everyone together in the middle carriages to keep warm.' Adam was talking as he hurried along the aisle. 'The driver's pretty poorly, and your girl Emma's with him in the front carriage. There's also a woman passenger who was hurt when the train stopped suddenly.'

Adam seemed capable and to have everything under control. Not easy on a train full of cold, frightened people and in virtual darkness, apart from the flickering emergency lights. 'I've been through and asked everyone if they're okay. There are a few cuts and bruises, but I let them stay in their seats. One of them's a child and her mother wanted to keep her away from the more serious injuries.'

Joe's voice sounded from behind Neve, calm and confident. 'That's good. Can you go round again? If anyone seems asleep and you can't wake them, or they seem disoriented, let us know. Sometimes adrenaline can mask shock or other injuries for a while.'

'Will do.' Adam held the connecting doors open for Neve, and she stepped through into the front carriage.

She could see Emma's face at the far end and walked towards her. A hand reached out from the darkness and grabbed her arm.

'You're the doctor. My wife's hurt…' A man had tight hold of her arm.

Joe was there. 'All right, mate.' His fingers curled around the man's wrist, applying brief pressure below the thumb, and the grip on her arm relaxed suddenly. 'I'll see your wife.'

She nodded at Joe, and made for the end of the carriage, not looking back. There was no choice now. Joe was going to have to come through for her.

The young woman was weeping softly, and a brief glance was enough to tell Joe what was wrong. Another woman, sitting next to her, was supporting her arm, stretched out awkwardly, to accommodate the metal spike that disappeared through a hole in her sleeve just below the elbow and seemed to be running straight through her arm.

'What's her name?' He turned to the woman's husband.

'Her name is Jan… You're a doctor?'

'Yes, Dr Joe Lamont. If I can just get a bit closer…' Joe craned over, training the light from his torch onto the spike, which he could now see was a knitting needle.

'Jan, my name's Joe. I'm a doctor.'

Her face was pale and her eyes red from crying, but she seemed alert enough. 'They said you were coming…'

The look in a person's eyes when they knew that they were hurt and that someone was there to help never failed to move Joe. 'I'm going to get a few things but I'll only be a moment. Then I'll take a proper look at your arm. Okay?'

'Yes. Thanks.'

At the other end of the carriage Neve was kneeling on

ANNIE CLAYDON

131

the floor, bent over a middle-aged man, who was lying on a makeshift bed made out of passengers' coats. She was talking quietly to him.

Joe puffed out a relieved breath. The man was obviously conscious, and it seemed that Neve had everything well under control. He quickly selected what he needed from her bag and, turning, nearly crashed into Jan's husband, who was hovering in the darkness behind him.

'Is there anything I can do?'

'Yeah. I want you to sit down opposite your wife. It'll hurt when I cut her sleeve, and she's going to need you there.'

He shepherded the man back up the carriage and slipped past him, carefully supporting Jan's arm while the woman who had been holding it ducked out of the way. Then he sat down next to Jan, training the light of his torch onto the knitting needle. It was bent from the impact that must have driven it through her arm, and Joe's initial plan was to leave it in situ.

'Okay, Jan, let's see if I can't make you a bit more comfortable before the ambulance gets here.' Joe smiled at her. 'First of all I want to check that you're not hurt anywhere else. Did you bump your head at all?'

'No.'

'Good. I'm going to open your coat and feel your tummy and legs. Just to make sure.' Joe was confident enough that Jan was able to tell him if she had any other injuries, but he wasn't going to leave it to chance.

Joe handed the torch over to the woman who had been supporting Jan's arm, and indicated where he wanted her to shine its beam. Putting on a pair of gloves, he opened Jan's coat, feeling her stomach, back and legs carefully, watching for any signs of pain and alert for the sticky feel of blood. 'Does this hurt?'

'No.'

He finished his careful probing and tucked Jan's coat back around her. 'Good. You're doing fine. I'm afraid I'm going to have to cut your sleeve so I can get a look at the wound now.'

'That's okay. I never much liked this coat.' Jan seemed calm enough, but Joe was watching her carefully. The emotional effect of seeing something passing through your own body wasn't something that it would be wise to ignore.

'I'm not going to touch the knitting needle yet. It's best to leave it where it is and let them remove it at the hospital.'

'Okay. It looks so weird, though…'

'I know. I want you to take your husband's hand and look at him. Can you do that?'

Jan summoned a smile. 'Yes, I can do that. The look of love, eh?'

Joe chuckled. 'That's right. Straight into his eyes.' Joe wondered what it would have been like if someone—who was he trying to kid?—if Neve had been there to hold his hand when he'd been hurt. Whether it would have made any difference at all.

'You think this is the time to mention our anniversary…?'

'I think it's an excellent time.' Joe's heart thumped in his chest. Jan knew beyond doubt that her husband was there for her, without having to ask or even think about it. It seemed to make all the difference to her.

'Anything you want, babe.' Jan's husband rallied, sliding forward in his seat and taking hold of her hand, and Jan turned her head towards him.

'Just you.' Jan silently mouthed the words and her husband gripped tight onto her hand.

Joe began to cut the thick woollen material of Jan's coat, carefully freeing it on both sides from the metal spike. Then the material underneath. The wound was oozing blood, but that was already beginning to congeal around the shaft of the knitting needle.

'We're good, Jan. It's not bleeding too much. I'm going to put padding around it to protect it a bit and stop it from moving.'

Jan shot him a teary smile. 'Thanks… It hurts pretty bad.'

'Yes, I know, and we're going to do something about that. I want you to sit tight, and I'll go and get some pain relief for you.' He slid out from his seat, indicating to Jan's husband exactly how he wanted him to support her arm while he was gone.

'Joe. Cardiac arrest…'

Neve's voice rose above the quiet voices in the carriage, and for a moment Joe froze. He'd been here before. Left one patient to tend to another, and that time he'd made the wrong choice. Suddenly the quiet, focussed confidence that had grown as he'd carefully tended to Jan shattered into smithereens.

'Joe…' Her voice again. Joe made his decision.

'Stay there. Just as you are.' Jan's husband gave him a quick nod. 'I'll be back as soon as I can.'

Neve was still kneeling on the floor next to her patient. Another young woman, who must be Emma, was shrinking back from them, her hand over her mouth in an expression of helpless horror. Joe ignored her for the moment, bending down next to Neve.

Suddenly everything came together. Like two parts of a machine, snapping into place and humming smoothly into life. Without a word, Joe lifted the man, supporting him while Neve snatched the cushions out from under him.

'How long…?'

'Twenty seconds. Start CPR.'

Joe was already there. 'Tell me you've got a defibrillator in your bag.'

'Yep. Emma, we need some light, please. Over here.'

There was no time to thank Joe for coming through for her. Gerry had been awake and talking when Neve had arrived, and suddenly this. His heart, already weakened by the heart attack, had stopped pumping blood, and he had begun to die before her eyes. Neve opened her medical bag and pulled out the defibrillator, taking the pads from their protective wrapper.

'Got a razor?' Joe had already got the coats covering Gerry out of the way, and bared his chest.

'Yep.' One glance told her that she was going to need it. Neve pulled the disposable razor from the side pocket of her bag, and while Joe continued CPR a few quick strokes of the razor made two patches in the dense mat of springy chest hair, large enough for the pads to stick properly.

'Ready for defibrillation.' The shorter the interruption in CPR, the better, and Joe needed to know exactly when to stop.

'Okay. On your call.' His voice was calm and steady.

'Checking… Stand clear.'

Joe moved back. 'Safe.'

Neve pushed the button and Gerry seemed to stiffen slightly. 'No response. Resume CPR.'

Joe clasped his hands again, pushing rhythmically on Gerry's chest, replicating the beat of a heart that currently wasn't capable of doing its job. The CPR would keep blood circulating around his body until the defibrillator could recharge and another shock be delivered.

'Ready.'

'Okay.'

'Checking… Stand clear.'

'Safe.'

The same smooth procedure. It was as if they'd planned it all in advance, choreographed each move. Somehow their training, undertaken on different sides of an ocean, and their experience, also different, dovetailed together in a smooth, unbroken pattern.

'I've got a normal sinus rhythm.'

A little choking sob came from behind her, and the beam of the torch quivered. Emma had done well but this was a lot for a twenty-year-old law student, whose only medical experience came second-hand from her father.

'It's okay, Emma.' Joe's voice, quiet and reassuring. 'You've done really well. Just give us another few minutes and then I promise you can fall apart. What's his name?'

'Gerry.' The light steadied as Emma took a deep breath and gulped back her tears.

'Thanks.' Joe bent over the man, whose eyelids were beginning to flutter. 'Gerry. Can you hear me, Gerry?'

There was no reply, but Gerry's eyes were open now and struggling to focus. 'Gerry. Just lie still now.'

Gerry's heart was beating now, the rhythm regular. Neve kept watch on the small monitor of the defibrillator while Joe put a cushion under Gerry's head, talking to him all the time, reassuring him.

'Give me the torch, Em.' Neve shot a smile towards Emma. 'And would you slide my medical bag over here, please?'

Emma did as she was asked. 'There you go.'

'Thanks.' Neve found the pulse oximeter, clipping it on to Gerry's finger to check the oxygenation level of his blood. She nodded with satisfaction. Not bad, considering what he'd just gone through. Minutes ticked by.

'Are you satisfied that he's stable?' Joe murmured the question for only Neve to hear.

'Cautiously.' No one was in a position for anything more than that at the moment. 'Why?'

'I've got a woman back there with a knitting needle stuck through her arm.'

'A what?'

'Yeah. I want to get her some pain relief.'

'Okay. Look in my bag. I have paracetamol, or morphine if that's not enough…' She was keeping her eyes on Gerry, not looking at Joe. If Joe had a case that needed morphine then he was going to have to handle that himself.

'Thanks. I think the paracetamol should be enough for now. Won't be long.'

'Right. And can you see if you can find out about the ambulance?' Gerry was back with them again, but he was very weak. Even if he maintained this improvement, they had a ninety-minute window to get him to hospital before he started to suffer irreversible complications.

'Will do.' She heard Joe get to his feet. Almost felt him walk away. It was a cold feeling, almost annihilating the calm confidence she'd felt when he'd been there by her side. Neve took a breath and concentrated on Gerry.

'How is the ambulance going to get to us?' Emma's face was pale in the torchlight. Joe had been gone for ten, precious minutes.

'They'll find a way, Em. We'll just keep things going here until they do. Right?'

Emma nodded. 'Yes. Should I hold his hand or something?'

'That would be good.' Emma needed something to do almost as much as Gerry needed the comfort. 'We need to keep him calm and quiet. Reassure him.'

Emma took Gerry's hand between hers. 'Gerry, it's Emma. Just lie still and rest. The doctor's here and you're going to be all right.'

It was a rash promise, and one that Neve didn't know

whether she was going to be able to keep. She saw Gerry's fingers curl around Emma's and prayed that she could.

She heard footsteps behind her and Joe knelt down next to her. 'The first ambulance is about five minutes away and there's another behind it.'

'How are they going to get to us?' Neve didn't much want to see Gerry being carried over the fields to the ambulance.

'They're coming via the road that runs along the other side of the tracks.'

'Isn't it blocked?'

'Yeah. But apparently they've got a snowplough with them.'

She felt the light touch of his hand on her back. Didn't he know that he'd lost the right to do that? All the same, she was glad of that small reassurance.

'How did they manage that?'

Something that looked like a smile tugged at his lips. 'Who knows? Just be thankful they did.'

In less than five minutes a commotion at the entrance to the carriage heralded the arrival of the ambulance crew. Neve got to her feet and quickly briefed the young, sandy-haired man who accompanied them and who had introduced himself as a doctor.

The EMTs were gently transferring Gerry to a carry-cot, wrapping him in blankets and clipping an oxygen mask in place.

'How's your route back out of here?' Neve asked the doctor.

'We managed to get pretty close. Your colleague's helping the railway guys to clear a path up the embankment for us.' He grinned at her.

Neve had wondered where Joe had disappeared to, supposing that he was keeping out of the way now that the ambulance had arrived. She should have known better.

'Ready to go?' One of the ambulancemen caught the young doctor's eye.

'Yes.' He consulted Neve's written notes, which detailed exactly which drugs she'd given Gerry, along with the readings she'd taken from the portable defibrillator. 'We're good.'

'Safe journey.' Neve slipped her hand into Emma's as they watched the ambulance crew carry the portable cot down the narrow aisle.

'Thanks. We'll be fine. We've got a clear route back again. Are you coming with us? There'll be a spare seat up front.'

'No, we've got people I need to stay with here.' She squeezed Emma's hand. 'Do you want to go, Em?'

'I'm staying too.' The look on her face was remarkably like Maisie's when she had something that she was determined to see through until the end. The young doctor's mouth curled into an easy smile, which was all for Emma.

Neve squeezed Emma's hand. 'Perhaps my colleague… Tell him that I said I can manage here now.' The intimacy of working with Joe to save a man's life had been fragile and transitory, over before Gerry had been strapped into the carry-cot. All the same, the thought that he would probably jump at the chance to be out of here made her feel suddenly cold.

'Okay, will do.' The doctor shot one last grin in Emma's direction and she returned the compliment. Then he hurried along the aisle to catch up with the ambulance crew. Neve swallowed the tears that sprang inexplicably to her eyes and focussed on the woman that Joe had seen halfway down the carriage. She still had a job to do.

CHAPTER FOURTEEN

NEVE TOOK A deep breath and approached the small group. 'Hi. My name's Neve. How are you doing?'

'Not so bad. How's that man?'

'Stable. The really good news is that he's on his way to hospital now. And the other piece of good news is that another ambulance should be here for you very soon.'

'Thanks.' The woman was obviously in pain but Joe had done a good job of making her comfortable, her arm supported on a couple of bags, cushioned with a soft jacket. She had a fire blanket over her, and when Neve touched her other hand, it was warm.

'Do you have any discomfort anywhere else, or is it just your arm?' She should check that nothing had been missed.

The woman's lips twitched into a smile. 'No, nothing else. Joe, the other doctor, asked me that, too, and checked me over.' She gave a shrug, wincing as the muscles of her shoulder pulled at her injured arm. She seemed bright enough. And the grin she'd given when she'd talked about Joe checking her over seemed a perfectly understandable reaction from a patient who was alert enough to appreciate it. Joe could be as professional as he liked, you still couldn't change human nature.

'How did you do it?' Neve carefully inspected the dressing for any signs of new bleeding.

'Jan was holding her knitting up, counting the rows, when the train stopped and she fell right onto the needle,' the man sitting next to her chipped in.

'Good thing it was just my arm.' Jan rolled her eyes. 'It was one hell of a jolt.'

Neve had noticed that the floor of the carriage was at a slight angle, and as soon as she got the chance she should ask exactly what had happened here. 'Joe's given you something for the pain?'

Jan smiled, reaching under the fire blanket and taking out a piece of thick card, trimmed to make a label and secured around her neck with strips of gauze and surgical tape. Clearly marked on the card were the time, date and the dose of paracetamol that Joe had given.

'Right. Looks as if all we need to do is wait for the ambulance, then.'

The second ambulance crew appeared in the doorway of the carriage a few minutes later. Jan was helped to her feet and secured in a carry-cot, and her husband shook Neve's hand before he left.

'Tell Joe thank you as well.'

'Yes, I will.' She probably wouldn't get the chance. Joe was gone now, and he wasn't coming back. Soon he'd be on his way back to Canada. Perhaps it was better this way. While Neve still had the other passengers on the train to think about, she couldn't curl up in a ball and cry. She took a deep breath and opened the connecting door into the second carriage, looking for Adam Grimshaw.

Expectant faces turned towards her. Then there was a murmur of conversation.

Someone started to clap. Then someone else. By the time she got to the centre of the carriage everyone was applauding. She wasn't as alone as she'd thought, but still the one person that she wanted wasn't here. Neve held up her hands for silence.

'Thanks, everyone. The two people who were hurt are on their way to hospital now…' She was interrupted by the murmur of approval which went around the carriage.

'When can we get out?' A man's voice from the corner.

'I don't know any more than you. I'll try to find out.'

'Can't we walk along the tracks? Go the same way that you came in?' Another voice.

'No.' Neve remembered what she'd heard from the TV about the dangers of passengers getting out of a stranded train. 'It's not safe. And, anyway, there's no transport. We'd be stuck miles from anywhere. If you think it's cold in here…'

A murmur ran around the carriage and then another voice rose above the rest. 'Best to stay here.'

One voice of sanity at least. A few others joined in, and the mood swung back in favour of staying put. Neve caught sight of Adam, entering the carriage from the other end, and hurried towards him.

'Did you get to check on everyone, as my colleague asked?'

'Yes. There are two more minor injuries for you to see. A woman with a swollen hand and the child. Do you want me to get them brought down to you?'

'Yes, as long as the front carriage is stable. It seems to be listing to one side…'

Adam nodded. 'The wheels of that carriage hit a lump of ice and slid off the rails. They're stuck fast now.'

'You're sure?' It all sounded a bit precarious to Neve. 'Is there any danger of the carriage tipping any further?'

'No, I've been down there and taken a look. The front wheels are wedged between two rails. That carriage, and the rest of the train for that matter, isn't going anywhere. We're working on evacuating into a rescue train.'

'Some of the passengers are talking about walking along the tracks. I said it was a really bad idea and that we should wait.'

Adam nodded. 'Yeah, thanks. If anyone else asks, stick to that message. It's much too dangerous to have a whole train full of people walking along live tracks. I've had some flasks of coffee sent along the line and hopefully that'll give everyone something else to think about.'

'Coffee?' Neve could really do with a cup of coffee right now, and she expected that Emma could too.

Adam grinned. 'I'll have a flask sent along to you straight away. It's the least I can do.' His face reddened slightly and he held out his hand to Neve. 'I've known Gerry for thirty years and he's a good mate. Thank you.'

Neve took his hand and he gripped hers tightly. 'I'm glad I was here to help.'

'I want to thank Emma too. There was no one on the train who had any medical knowledge, and she stepped forward like a good 'un, even though she was shaking like a leaf.'

Tears brimmed in Neve's eyes at the thought of Emma, afraid and alone. At least she had her training and experience to guide her. 'I'm just going to talk to her now. She's a bit shaken up, and if you have a minute I'd be really glad if you could say a few words to her.'

'It'll be my privilege to shake that girl's hand.' Adam seemed to realise that he still had hold of Neve's, and let it go suddenly. 'I'll go and get the coffee and I'll be right there.'

When Neve re-entered the front carriage, Emma was sitting on her own at the far end of the carriage, hugging her coat around her tightly, her face streaked with tears. Neve made a beeline for her.

'Hey, Em.' She sat down next to her, putting her arm around her shoulders.

Emma nodded an acknowledgement. 'Where's Joe?'

'He's gone with the ambulance.' Neve heard her voice break slightly.

'Do you think Gerry's going to be all right?'

'He's on his way to hospital.'

Emma quirked her mouth downwards. 'I didn't know what to do, Neve.'

'That's okay. You kept your head, and you called for help. Then you did what your dad told you until Joe and I got there. That was more than enough.'

'But if I'd been able to see the signs perhaps I could have done something earlier so he didn't go into cardiac arrest…'

'Em, listen.' Neve took Emma firmly by the shoulders. The girl knew just enough to realise what was happening and to blame herself for it. 'Gerry's heart was weakened by the heart attack and that's what precipitated the arrest. There was nothing you could have done. The only reason that Joe and I got here in time was because of you.'

'I'm going to learn how to do CPR.' Emma's voice was small, but a note of determination had crept into it.

'That's a good idea. Everyone should.'

Emma nodded, wiping her face with her hand. 'Perhaps Joe will teach me.'

'Perhaps he will.' Unlikely. Unless he and Emma could fit the lessons in some time in the next few days before he left.

'Perhaps I will what?'

A deep voice sounded behind them. Neve didn't dare look up.

'Joe! You came back!' Emma didn't have any of Neve's hesitation in expressing her joy.

'Of course.'

'I thought you'd gone with the ambulance.' Neve heard her voice shake. Her heart had wanted him there so badly, even though her head had patiently explained that it wouldn't be for long and that there would only be more tears when he did leave.

'I was on the embankment, helping the crews up with the carry-cots.' He smiled at Neve, and then turned the voltage up to full when he grinned at Emma. 'How's it going, Em?'

'We're glad to see you.' Emma sprang to her feet and delivered the hug that Neve hadn't offered. Joe held her tight, his hands spread across her back. Neve knew how reassuring that felt. It would be downright mean-spirited to begrudge Emma that comfort.

She saw Adam at the entrance to the carriage, carrying a flask and some polystyrene cups. 'Why don't you go and get some coffee, Em? I think that Adam wants a word with you.'

'Oh. Coffee.' Fortified by the hug, and the thought of a hot drink, Emma started to pick her way down the aisle to the other end of the carriage, leaving Joe and Neve alone.

Neve reckoned he would probably find something else pressing to do now, something that would discreetly avoid the need for any conversation between them. But instead he sat down opposite her.

'What's that all about?' He nodded towards Emma's receding back.

'Adam wanted to thank her personally for coming forward to help.' She twisted round in her seat, watching as Adam took Emma's hand and shook it, receiving a brilliant smile in return.

When she turned back towards Joe he was nodding in approval. 'She deserves a bit of recognition. This must have been very difficult for her.'

'Yes, it was. And for you, too. Thanks for being here, Joe.'

He leaned forward, propping his elbows on his knees.

Joe had a knack of conjuring up their own little world, making it seem as if they were alone in a crowd. Shielded by the high backs of the seats, it was as if there wasn't another person for miles.

'I don't deserve any thanks. I almost didn't come.'

'I know. But you did come, and you made all the difference. That's what matters, not what you almost did.'

For a moment that precious connection flashed between them, as if it had never been broken. Then he shook his head. 'You know there's more to it than that, Neve.'

'I know that I didn't give you much encouragement.' Neve didn't want to think about what the consequences of her own angry pride might have been.

'You called me.'

'I hung up on you.'

'You had every right to be angry. Anyone who thinks that saving a life isn't appropriate isn't worth much.'

'Anyone who gets over their own personal feelings and does the right thing is worth something. Worth a great deal, actually.' Joe had hurt her badly but lashing out like a wounded animal wasn't going to help either of them. He deserved better than that, and the thought occurred to Neve that maybe she did too.

'I'll remember that. Next time I manage to get myself into this kind of situation…'

She twisted her mouth. 'Which I imagine is going to be a very long time in the future, if you've got any say in the matter.'

A short burst of wry laughter. 'Yeah. Probably.'

'In the meantime, remember this. Gerry. He's the guy you helped save. Remember his name.'

He swept his hand across his eyes, as if he suddenly felt weary. 'Will you do me a favour?'

'Depends what it is.' Making up your mind to act like

an adult only extended so far. The fragile, uneasy truce between them could only stand so much pressure.

His gaze focussed on hers, and heat seared through her senses. 'You're a great doctor and… Next time anyone tells you that you need to change, could you just laugh in their face, please?'

'I'll think about it.'

He nodded. 'Okay. That's good enough.'

There weren't going to be any next times for her and Joe. He wasn't going to say that he'd suddenly seen the light, that his confidence had been restored and he was taking up medicine again. He wasn't going to believe that they could try again. Miracles like that didn't happen. Not in a matter of days at least, and in a few days' time he'd be on a plane on his way back to Canada.

'Emma…thanks.' He stood suddenly, and Neve turned round to see Emma, balancing three polystyrene cups of coffee, each perched on the lid of the other. He lifted one out and handed it to Neve.

'Ah. Thanks. I could do with that.' The chill in the carriage was beginning to work its way back into her bones. 'Have they brought our next patients through yet?'

'They're on their way. In fact, the first one's here now.' Emma grinned at her.

'I'll go.' Joe signalled towards the other end of the carriage that he'd be right there. 'Sit for a minute and drink your coffee. I'll call you if I need you.'

Neve sipped her drink, smiling as Emma proudly told her what Adam had said to her. She was unable to sit still for very long, though. And when she stood up she was drawn to Joe, as if by some irresistible magnetic force.

He was sitting at the other end of the carriage next to a young woman, a little girl of about three on his lap. He was persuading his young patient that having the small cut on her arm cleaned wasn't so bad after all.

'First I'm going to clean your arm with this, Daisy.' Joe had an antiseptic wipe from Neve's medical bag in his hand, and Daisy took it from him, rubbing it onto the sleeve of his jumper.

'No, honey, on the skin.' Joe pulled up his sleeve, his arms still around Daisy. She responded to his prompt and scrubbed mercilessly at his forearm.

'Ow…' He gave a little grimace of mock pain. 'It stings a bit, but that's because it's working properly.'

He pulled another wipe from the packet and Daisy smiled up at him. 'Snap…'

'Of course. I forgot that.' He snapped the edge of one of the surgical gloves he was wearing against his wrist. 'Ready now?'

Daisy nodded. Joe started to clean the wound gently, holding her tight when she squirmed and whimpered a little. 'I'm sorry, honey. Nearly finished.'

It was almost too much to bear. The tenderness. The softness of a child against the war-torn ruggedness of the man. The final straw was that Daisy looked a little like Joe, dark hair and big brown eyes. He'd make a great father…

You're out of order… She had no right to even think that. Absolutely no right to pretend that Joe wanted the same as her. He had his own life, his own aspirations, and they had nothing in common with her own.

'You're a very brave girl, Daisy. Now I'm going to put a little sticky plaster on the cut, which you mustn't take off…' He showed her the stitch. 'It doesn't hurt.'

'Snap!'

'That's right. Thanks for reminding me.' Joe snapped the surgical gloves again, and Daisy laughed up at him. This was torture.

He decided on two stitches, clearly veering towards the safe side. He applied them so swiftly, so expertly that

Daisy hardly blinked. 'Now I'm going to put a bandage over the top, just to keep everything in place…'

That was it. Neve couldn't watch any more. Adam was guiding a middle-aged woman through into the carriage, holding her bags for her, and Neve turned and plastered a bright smile on her face to greet them.

CHAPTER FIFTEEN

Now that there was nothing to do but wait, time seemed to slow to an interminable crawl. Joe had responded to Daisy's demands for a story and then delivered her back into her mother's arms. Neve was busy with a woman who looked as if she had a sprained wrist, and Emma was sitting at the far end of the carriage with her nose in a book.

Seized with restless energy born of dissatisfaction with the world rather than enthusiasm for the job in hand, he walked to the other end of the train to liaise with Adam and see whether he could get any reception on his phone. Two bars was a hollow victory, because there was no one he wanted to call. It seemed that everything he'd ever wanted was right here. Close enough to touch, but not his to take.

'What's the story, then?' It was Emma who caught Joe's attention when he walked back into the front carriage, his heart grumbling with discontent.

'It'll be a while.' He threw himself down in the seat opposite Emma and Neve. 'Hello, there, sweetheart...'

Emma was struggling to hold Daisy on her lap as the child reached for him, and Joe felt a sharp, instinctive tug of warmth.

'Here, you take her. She doesn't want me any more.' Emma grinned, lifting Daisy across the small table between them, and the little girl reached for him with an eagerness that almost shattered his heart.

Her hands were a little cold, and Joe unzipped his jacket, letting Daisy snuggle into his body heat. Maybe she needed her mother…

'I want a story.' Daisy's mother was deep in conversation at the other end of the carriage, and her gaze flicked up automatically at the sound of her child's voice. Then she smiled at Joe and turned back to the woman with the injured wrist, obviously reckoning that he was the man for that particular job.

'Okay, Daisy. What about the one about the penguin and the polar bear?'

Emma giggled. 'Aren't penguins at the North Pole? And polar bears at the South?'

'Other way round. That's the whole point of the story.' Joe hadn't dared look at Neve, but now he chanced a quick glance. She was staring fixedly out of the window at the dark walls of the tunnel.

'Hmm. Talking about impossible treks, is there any news about when we'll get out of here? Or are they going to send turkey sandwiches and candles down the line for tomorrow?' Emma grinned at him. 'Or perhaps *we* could walk home.'

Joe rolled his eyes. 'We can't walk along the line, Em.'

'How dangerous can it be? You and Neve did it.'

Neve seemed to wake from her reverie at the sound of her name. 'We walked a few yards in order to get here in an emergency. It's miles to the station behind us, and to get to Leminster we'd have to walk through the tunnel ahead, in the dark.'

'All right, so we can't move, and we can't walk. What *can* we do?' Emma stirred restlessly, and Daisy turned her big brown eyes onto Joe.

'They're backing a rescue train down the track towards

us. It'll get as close as possible to the front of the train, and
we'll all walk through into it. Then it's just a few minutes
to Leminster station.'

'So it won't be long, then?' Neve was looking at him
now, her eyes suddenly filled with tears.

'No. Not long.' It was Joe's turn to avert his gaze. He
got to his feet, taking Daisy with him, and started to walk
along the carriage. 'This story's about a penguin and a
polar bear, and a very, very long walk.'

It was almost an hour before Joe heard the sound of ac-
tivity coming from the front of the train, which signalled
that the rescue train had arrived. It took another half an
hour to manoeuver it into position and rig up a walkway
between the trains. When the time came to evacuate the
carriages, everyone queued quietly, waiting their turn for
the railway staff to help them across the gap. Joe carried
Daisy across and, with a trace of reluctance transferred
her into the arms of her mother on the other side.

There was another wait while the walkway was disman-
tled, but at least this train was warm and there were hot
drinks, sandwiches and unblocked toilets. Finally the train
started to move slowly up the track to Leminster station.

When they arrived everyone made a beeline for the
warmth of the waiting room, where a surprising number
of people were gathered, waiting for the train to arrive.
Joe hung back, watching while Neve made sure that the
woman with the sprained wrist and Daisy's mother both
had someone to take them home.

Emma had someone too. A greying, middle-aged man
broke his way through the crowd, and Emma fell into her
father's arms, talking volubly. The man listened, pride and
relief shining from his face when he looked at his daughter,
and Joe looked away, suddenly feeling as if he was being
intrusive. This was their world, not his.

For a moment Neve was alone at the station. No one had come for her. He watched as she shouldered her bag and began to walk slowly towards the exit.

Neve's face hurt from smiling, and her heart hurt from pretending to everyone who wished her a happy Christmas that she too was looking forward to tomorrow. It was time for her to get going. It was already dark and she had a long walk ahead of her.

'Neve! Wait!' Ted's voice rang out, and Neve turned to see him hurrying towards her, his arm wrapped protectively around Emma.

'Thank you for everything, Neve. Maisie sends her love, too.' Ted's look said it all. It wasn't just Gerry who had needed saving. Emma had been spared the agony of having to watch a man die and being able to do nothing about it.

'I'm glad I was there.' Ted raised his eyebrows in disbelief and Neve grinned at him. 'Well, you know…'

'I know.' Suddenly she was no longer the most junior doctor in the practice, in need of support and guidance. She was an equal, who had done her job well and gained his respect. 'We'll give you a lift home.'

'That's okay. It'll take you out of your way and it's going to take ages. Probably quicker if I walk.'

'Not in the dark and with that heavy bag.' Ted's decision on this was obviously final.

'Perhaps you can just put my bag in the boot of your car. I'll drop by and collect it after Christmas.'

'I'm taking you.' Joe's voice boomed out from behind her and Neve jumped. If only he'd stop creeping up behind her…

She should be careful what she wished for. Joe almost certainly wasn't going to be doing it again. It was tough to creep up behind someone from a different continent.

'Joe Lamont?' Ted stretched his free hand out towards

Joe and the men shook hands. 'Ted Johnstone…I'm Emma's father. Pleased to meet you. My wife's been singing your praises.'

'My car's five minutes down the road. I've just checked with the station staff, and the trains down to London are still running.' Joe was looking at Neve.

Ted brightened. 'In that case, we won't keep you. Travel safely, eh?'

'Er…yes, I will.' Neve was about to protest that she wasn't going anywhere with Joe, but that would mean that Ted would insist on taking her home. Get one good Samaritan out of the way at a time.

Happy Christmases were wished all around, and Ted turned, hurrying Emma to his car, his arm still firmly around her. Joe picked up Neve's medical bag and started to walk, realising after a few steps that she wasn't with him.

'What?' He turned and faced her.

'I don't need a lift, Joe. I'm going home.'

'Yeah, we'll pop in at your place, collect your bags…' He stopped suddenly. 'You've no intention of going down to London tonight, have you?'

'It's too late. The local train services are probably disrupted and it'll take me for ever.'

'I'll take you over to Leeds and you can get the intercity train from there.'

He still hadn't given up on the hope that Neve had successfully managed to put aside hours ago. 'I appreciate it, Joe. But I'd have to go back home and get my things, and then goodness only knows how long it'd take to get to Newcastle. It's too late. I'd rather stay here.'

'I'm happy to try. If there's a chance…'

'There's no chance.' Joe was just clutching at straws, and even if there had been some chance of her getting down to London, Neve wouldn't have gone with him. The grim perversity of wishing he was there when he wasn't and then, when he appeared, wishing he'd go away had to stop. She had to say goodbye to him and mean it.

He thought for a moment. 'All right, then. I'll take you home.' Neve opened her mouth to protest and he held one hand up to silence her.

'Don't make a liar out of me, Neve. Ted only left you behind here because he thought that I was driving you. I know you think you can manage everything by yourself, and if anyone can then it's you. But, just this once, you're coming with me, if I have to sling you over my shoulder and carry you.'

He wouldn't. Neve looked at his face, set with determination, and decided that he probably would. He certainly could, she knew just how strong Joe was. And he didn't seem to appreciate the irony of his insisting that she get home safely and then breaking her heart all over again by leaving her there.

'Okay. But you take me home and then you go.' Somehow it didn't seem so bad when she was in control of things.

'All right.' He turned and started to walk again, and this time Neve followed him.

Joe hadn't wanted any of this. He would have driven her all the way to London, rather than take her back to her dark, silent house to spend the rest of Christmas Eve alone. But Neve didn't want that.

And that was what it all boiled down to. She didn't want what he could give. He couldn't give what she wanted. It was a hundred per cent or nothing, and even his craving for what might be didn't make any difference. If there was any chance that he couldn't make her dreams come true, he had to hit the road.

The quickest route from the station to his car, parked

outside his cottage, was along a footpath that skirted the
back of Leminster High Street. She'd begun to drop back
a little, unable to keep up the pace, and Joe stopped to wait
for her. 'Okay?'

'Yeah.' She was too breathless to furnish any further
detail.

The almost magnetic effect that being close to Neve
exerted on him threatened to pull him closer to her. It took
physical effort to maintain a safe distance. As they trudged
towards his car he noticed that it was a perfect Christmas
Eve, the sky above them clear and full of stars, and that
somehow even that meant absolutely nothing to him.

'Get in while I clear the windscreen.' He called to her
and she ignored him. Being ignored by Neve was better
than making love to any other woman he'd known before.

Together, they cleared the fresh snow from the car. Even
that wasn't easy. Working silently together, alone in the
empty street, he still felt as if these moments were golden,
because Neve was there. It was a final, slightly unlikely
confirmation of his resolve. He was leaving, and the sooner
he went, the better.

Walking alone up the path of her house and slipping the
key into her front door had been the final straw. After everything they'd been through today, Joe had stayed res-
olutely in the driver's seat, not even moving to help her
with her bag.

The house was cold and dark. Neve and Joe had fallen
apart before he'd had the chance to pick her up that Christmas tree he mentioned, and since she hadn't planned to
be here, she'd given the rest of the festive decorations a
miss too. She dropped her bag in the hallway, texted her
parents to tell them what had happened and not to expect
her, and went upstairs, leaving her coat on the floor in the
hallway outside the bathroom door. Sighing, she began to

run a hot bath in the hope that it might dispel the chill in her bones and the ache in her limbs.

The hot water was soothing but did nothing for the ache in her heart. If Joe couldn't relent on Christmas Eve, he wasn't going to. That was that. End of story.

She was just beginning to relax when her phone rang. Neve scattered water everywhere, getting out of the bath by the third ring and extracting the phone from her coat pocket by the fifth. 'Yes…?' She was shivering and naked in the hall, hoping against shattered hope…

'Neve…? Where are you?' Maisie's voice on the line dashed that hope.

'I was in the bath. Hold on, Maisie.' Neve hurried back into the warm bathroom, wrapped a towel around her and made for her bedroom. 'I'm back. Sorry about that.'

'Ted said that you were going home tonight. What happened?'

'I decided it was too late.' Too late for a lot of things. Much too late to expect that every time the phone rang it was going to be Joe.

'I wish you'd said. He could have brought you over here tonight.' Reproof sounded in Maisie's voice. 'He'll come over and pick you up…'

'No, thanks, Maisie, I just want an early night.'

'In that case, you're coming to us tomorrow. No arguments.'

'I appreciate the offer but—'

'We'll pick you up tomorrow morning. I'll give you a call around ten to see what time suits you.'

It was time to give it up. Joe wasn't going to call or drop by, and there was no point in staying here, wishing he would. It was time to get on with her life.

'Maisie, I don't know what to say…' Suddenly Maisie's kindness made Neve want to cry.

'It's easy. Just say yes. And that you'll be awake by ten, when I call you.'

'That'll be great, Maisie. Thanks so much.'

Neve ended the call and put the phone down next to her on the bed. It was Christmas after all. Maybe not the one she wanted, but she had friends and she was going to make the best she could of it.

CHAPTER SIXTEEN

CHRISTMAS MORNING. You couldn't stay in bed on Christmas morning, even if there weren't presents or family waiting for you. Neve got up early, slipping on a pair of socks and a thick cardigan over her pyjamas, and padded downstairs to the kitchen. Two shots of espresso, with a small spoon of grated chocolate, fluffed milk and nutmeg. That would start the day right.

She sat down at the kitchen table, making herself comfortable, for the first sip of coffee. Closed her eyes and tried to believe that it tasted like heaven when all it really tasted of was pain. Perhaps some carols. She reached for the radio and fiddled with the dial.

A quiet scrape at the front door. She wouldn't have heard it if she hadn't failed to find anything that sounded festive enough on the radio, had set it to retune and was waiting while it searched all available stations. She wouldn't have wandered out into the hall to peer through the letterbox and see what was going on out there.

Her view was obscured by a branch. It didn't look like any of the shrubs in her small front garden and it was unlikely that any of the trees in the lane had blown over. She fiddled with the latch and opened the door.

The first thing she saw was a large Christmas tree, almost filling the small porch. The next was Joe, sitting in his car, the engine running and ready to go. When he caught sight of her, the look on his face would have done credit to a six-year-old caught feeding the goldfish to next-door's cat.

'I've left you a few things.' He gestured towards the tree. Neve took a step forward and almost fell over a couple of cardboard boxes, which were blocking her exit from the house.

'What? Joe…?'

He waved, in an uncharacteristic show of Christmas jocularity. 'Got to get on. Happy Christmas.' With that, the car window slid upwards and Joe started to drive away slowly.

That must be the way he wanted it. The sudden pain in her chest, the feeling that she couldn't breathe, made her choke.

'Joe!' She didn't stop to think. There was no point, the sudden jolt of sheer emotion made thought impossible. Shoving the boxes out of the way, Neve took the front path at a run. She was in the lane, calling his name, before she even felt the bite of the cold.

The car skidded to a halt. Joe was out of the driver's seat and powering towards her, and all she could feel was happiness.

'What the hell do you think you're doing?' He scooped her up in his arms, striding back towards the house. This was all that mattered. This moment. Everything else could go hang. She was where she wanted to be.

She was beginning to shiver as Joe kicked the front door closed behind him and carried her through to the kitchen. He was bristling with anger and somehow even that was bliss. Dumping her on the sofa, he knelt down in front of her, stripping off her wet socks and glaring at her feet.

'Well? What *did* you think you were doing? Don't you know that you can get frostbite in your toes even after a couple of minutes' exposure?' It appeared that his earlier question hadn't been purely rhetorical.

Shame, because she didn't have an answer, and the feeling that she'd just made a complete idiot of herself was tearing the fleeting happiness she'd felt to shreds.

'I could ask you the same thing. What's the idea of leaving stuff on my doorstep and then just driving away?' Neve snatched her foot away from him, tucking it up under her.

He looked up, his face clouded with doubt. 'I knew you didn't have a tree. I thought you might be pleased.'

'Oh, really. So you think it's okay to sleep with me then walk out on me and then just keep popping up again, offering me lifts, bringing me Christmas trees. It really is too much, Joe.'

'You were the one who called *me* yesterday morning, if I remember correctly.'

'I had an emergency on my hands. What was I supposed to do? And I didn't call you this morning.'

His brow darkened. 'Well, you'll just have to forgive me for caring about you.'

They glared at each other and finally Joe broke eye contact. 'You're right. I shouldn't have done it. You told me that if I left I wasn't to come back and I should have respected your wishes. I'm sorry.'

He picked up his gloves from the floor and got to his feet. She'd done it again. Said her piece and Joe had listened and was doing exactly as she'd told him and walking away. It was time to forget about pride, forget about making a point or being right. It was time to ask for what she wanted, however much it cost her.

Neve stumbled to her feet and took a few unsteady steps, grabbing hold of the kitchen table to support her. 'Joe, please stay a while.'

'I can't.'

'Dammit, Joe. I need you to stay. I'm begging you.'

He turned, the look on his face mirroring Neve's own shock at her outburst. A pulse beat at the side of his brow. 'Neve, you said it yourself. We can both see that this isn't going to work.'

'How can I see anything when you won't talk to me? Just talk to me Joe. Please.'

Talking wasn't going to do any good. It would just rip the wounds open, and change nothing in the process. But he'd already managed to prove that he couldn't stay away from her, even when she'd told him not to come back. Now that she'd begged him to stay, there was no way that he could leave.

'Sit down. Please, Joe.'

He'd never really been able to refuse her anything. Joe dropped his gloves on a chair and took his coat off. 'Here, finish your...' He caught the scent from the mug sitting on the table and recoiled. 'What on earth is that?'

'Chocolate, coffee and nutmeg. With frothed milk.' She sat down on the chair nearest the stove, holding her hands and feet towards its warmth. 'It's nice.'

'I'll take your word for that.' He handed her the concoction and she took a sip. 'What do you want to talk about?'

'I want you to tell me what happened to you, Joe. You won't practise as a doctor any more, you won't even try to make a commitment to me. I want to know why.'

'And if I tell you that I don't want to talk about it?' Joe knew that it wouldn't change anything.

'I'll say that you've taken my life and turned it upside down. I think I've got a right to know what it is that's keeping you from me.'

'It's best this way...' Joe repeated the words that he'd hung onto for the last week.

'How can I understand that? Don't you respect me

enough to at least tell me why? I deserve that, at least, don't I?'

She was honest and brave. At that moment Joe admired her more than anyone he knew. 'Yeah. You deserve that.'

He got up from his seat, walking over to the sink to get himself a glass of water. Something to relieve the parched feeling in his throat. Neve waited, still and silent.

'I was attached to a peacekeeping force, working as a surgeon in a field hospital. We saw all kinds of injuries, and we treated civilians who were caught up in the fighting, as well as our own troops. We'd been working for twenty-four hours straight when a new set of casualties were brought in. There was a local woman among them. She'd been sedated and had shrapnel in her leg.'

Neve nodded. Joe took another sip of water.

'I examined her quickly myself and read the notes. Then I made a decision that I would take another of the casualties into Theatre first. His wounds were potentially life-threatening and the woman seemed stable. I was wrong. She had internal injuries that had been missed on the first examination. She died on my operating table.'

Neve was blinking back tears. 'Joe, that's desperately sad. But it wasn't your fault, you had to rely on the information that you were given by the other people in your team. We all do.'

'It was my unit. My decision not to take her into surgery immediately. How would you have felt?'

Neve pursed her lips in thought. She had to be honest with him. 'Yes, I guess I would have felt responsible, too. It doesn't mean that you were. Was there any kind of inquiry?'

'I was exonerated of any blame.'

'Then don't you think that's something you should take into account?'

Joe knew just what she was thinking. His own words

came back to haunt him, echoing in his head. 'You mean that I should listen to my own words of wisdom—that it can take time for emotions to catch up with facts?'

'It's a thought. I know this is hard, Joe, and I won't for one minute pretend it's not a tragedy, but…well, losing patients does come with the territory.'

'This time it was different.'

'I don't understand…' She broke off suddenly, as if something had just occurred to her. 'What did this have to do with you being injured?'

'A couple of days later I went to see the family. I went alone, which was against regulations but I wanted to explain…somehow. Her father and mother agreed to meet me, and they listened to what I had to say. When I left the house I was surrounded by a crowd of people. Later I was told that the woman's brothers had found out that I was there and had come to demand justice.'

'What…what kind of justice?' Joe saw that Neve's hand was shaking.

'The kind that…' He shrugged. 'There were some punches thrown and I tried to get back to my vehicle. Some pushing and shoving, and I stumbled. Someone swung a baseball bat and I heard…felt…a crack…'

Her hand flew to her mouth. 'Your leg.'

'Yeah. At first I thought I'd just fallen and that I couldn't get up again…' Joe felt the panic rise in his chest.

'Okay.' Her hands were in his now and he held them tightly. 'It's okay, Joe. I'll help you.'

He hung onto her, trying desperately to regain control. Trying to forget the dark images that had plagued his dreams.

'They must have kicked you to rupture your spleen.' He heard her voice, quiet and soft, bringing him back to the here and now.

'Yeah.'

'And the kidney failure. That was a result of a blow?'

'More than one.'

She nodded. 'The scars around your shoulders look like wounds from a sharp knife that's been used to slash, not stab.' Her hands were shaking almost as much as his were, and they were both hanging onto each other, trying to get through this.

'Yeah. That's right.' He made an attempt at a joke. 'You're pretty good at this. Ever thought about forensics?'

'One day maybe *you'll* tell me everything. From beginning to end.'

He'd wanted to spare her that but she already knew most of it from the scars. One day maybe he would be able to tell it all. That day wasn't going to be soon, and when it came he'd be back in Canada.

'Have you considered that maybe the symptoms of PTSD have fed your guilt over this woman's death? That the two together have caught you in a trap, unable to move on?'

It had taken Joe a while to work that one out, and Neve had thought it through almost immediately. 'Yeah. But it doesn't make any difference, Neve. Whatever the reasons, I still can't make any promises to you. I'm still not someone that you should be involved with.'

Neve had planned everything out so well. Find someone, fall in love. Make a home, have children. It had seemed like a smooth progression, one leading seamlessly on to the next. But that might never happen with Joe, and if she wanted him she was going to have to take the biggest risk of her life.

'Joe, if you don't want me, then you should tell me...'

He tightened his grip on her hands. 'It's never been a matter of not wanting you, Neve.'

'Then I'll tell you what *I* want. I want a family, a career, a nice home. Most of all I want someone to love…'

'It's not me, Neve…' Pain brimmed in his eyes.

'Let me be the judge of that. I want you, Joe. Maybe things won't work out between us. I'm going into this with my eyes open and I can take that risk. What I can't live with is not even giving it a try.'

There. She'd said it. It seemed as if a great weight had been lifted off her shoulders.

'But…all that you went through with your ex-husband. I can't do that again to you, Neve.'

'Let me tell you what I went through with Matthew. I lost touch with who I was, and what I really wanted, because everything was all about what he wanted. I'm not going to let that happen again. This is what *I* want, and whatever you say isn't going to change my mind.'

'Neve…' He was lost for words. Seemed only to be able to say her name. It was like the sweet aftermath of their lovemaking. 'Neve.'

'What do you say? It's not going to be easy.'

'No. I guess it's not.'

She grinned at him. 'It'll be sweet…'

Joe's sudden smile. The one that came out of nowhere and hit you like a cannonball. 'I have absolutely no doubt of that.'

'Then can't we just try?'

He thought for long moments. Neve knew Joe well enough to know that if he said yes he meant it and he'd committed himself. This was going to be hard, for both of them, and he had to think it through.

'I think…if we decide to do it, we should go slowly.'

'Yes. I think we should.' Their first two weeks had been a whirlwind of emotion, neither of them stopping to really think about the consequences of their actions. Maybe that was why it had all fallen apart.

'I mean…' He grinned. 'I'm going to hate myself for saying this but…I think we should just concentrate on sharing some of the practical things at first. If that works then maybe sleeping together might come later…'

'You think you're going to hate yourself? *I* hate you for saying it.' She loved him for saying it. Sex had never been the problem. It was the sharing, the trust, the everyday intimacies they needed to work on.

He chuckled. 'Am I right, though?'

'Yeah. You're right.' Neve leaned towards him. 'I guess for the time being we can pass the time on these long winter nights by talking, eh?'

'There's a lot we still have left to say.' His dark gaze searched her face. 'Are you really okay with this, Neve? I have to know.'

Joe was nothing if not a gentleman. She liked that about him. Liked that he wanted to wait a little, until they'd both absorbed everything that had happened this morning.

'Yes, I am. As long as I don't have to wait too long.' She gave him her sweetest smile.

He chuckled. 'What have I let myself in for?'

'Well, someone's left a tree on my doorstep. You could get some exercise by carrying it through for me.'

'Can't manage by yourself?' He was teasing now.

'Yes, of course I can. But I've got to go upstairs and get dressed, and I don't want you to get bored while I'm gone. So if you could set it up just there…' She indicated a spot by the sofa, next to the old fireplace.

'Yes, ma'am.' His lips curled into a smile.

CHAPTER SEVENTEEN

JOE ROLLED UP his sleeves and got to work. Today hadn't exactly gone to plan so far, but he felt freer than he had in a long time. As if the world had opened up, and the possibilities that he had refused to acknowledge were...just that. Possibilities. Untested, but shining and new, like the fragile Christmas ornaments on a tree.

By the time Neve reappeared, pink and glowing from the shower and sporting a red sweater with holly motifs in honour of the day, he'd got the tree set up by the hearth and was carefully winding the lights around it, making sure that they were spaced evenly.

'Wow! It's a beautiful tree!'

Joe stood back and admired the thick, green branches. He'd taken a while that morning, tramping across the frozen ground to choose the best tree in the dim morning light, before he'd got to work with the chainsaw. Now that the tree was inside, he was satisfied with his choice.

'Glad you like it.'

'How did you know I didn't have one already?' She narrowed her eyes. She'd obviously been working through the practicalities in her head.

'You really want to know?' Of course she did. 'All right, I stopped the car last night and walked back. Looked through your sitting-room window.' Joe tried to make it sound like something that anyone would do, on any night of the year.

Her hand flew to her mouth. 'You did not! What would you have done if I'd had one in here?'

'I looked through the kitchen window as well.'

'Oh. So you've been sneaking around my house, peering through the windows…' Her blue eyes were teasing him. 'Then you went out this morning and chopped down a tree?'

'I called Frank Somersby last night and asked if I could have one of the conifers he grows for the Christmas market. Then I went out this morning and chopped it down.'

'And you left it on my doorstep. What was I supposed to think, that Father Christmas had been in the night?'

'I was going to text you.'

She laughed. 'Ah. Well, that's okay, then.' She bent to examine the boxes that he'd brought in from the doorstep. 'Decorations as well. You are so organised.'

'I had them in the cupboard. I was going to get a tree but, to tell you the truth, I didn't feel much like celebrating anything this last week.'

For a moment he thought she was going to kiss him. But instead she straightened, looking around as if something was missing. 'I'll put the kettle on.'

'Yeah? What do we need hot water for?'

She rolled her eyes. 'We have coffee and mince pies while we're decorating. Don't you know anything? Only we'll have to make do with biscuits, I haven't got any mince pies…'

That he could arrange. Joe opened the second box, and reached inside. 'Here.'

It was only a packet of shop-bought mince pies, but she received them as if they were the crown jewels.

'You think of everything! I'll put them into the oven for ten minutes to warm.' She bustled over to the stove and started to arrange the mince pies on a baking tray. 'Don't just stand there. Start laying the decorations out…'

Their first tree together. And the faint possibility of a repetition next year, sparkling insistently in his future. Suddenly it was all that Joe wanted, and getting this right was all-important. 'Okay, and then?'

'We start with the largest baubles, and work our way down to the smaller ones.'

'There's a procedure, then.' Joe had reckoned on just hanging them all on the tree, in whichever order they presented themselves.

'Of course there is. So don't just stand there…'

Decorating the tree had always been one of those enjoyable Christmas traditions that Joe's parents had demanded he and his four brothers attend. But it had never been delightful. Magical. Full of joy, with a final burst of euphoria, as Joe lifted Neve up to place the sparkling, golden star at the top of the tree.

'It's beautiful!' He'd been loath to let her go, and when he set her back down again Joe had absent-mindedly left his arm wrapped around her waist.

He nodded with approval. 'Not so bad.'

Her elbow found his ribs. 'Not so bad? It's wonderful. Now the lights…'

He was torn between keeping her close and seeing her face when he switched the lights on. But she was practically running on the spot with excitement, and this was everything he'd wanted for her this Christmas. Joe plugged in the lights and flipped the switch, and she did a little dance of pleasure, clapping her hands with glee.

'It's beautiful. Isn't it beautiful?'

He was all done with understatement. 'Yeah. Beautiful.' Joe wondered if she knew that the observation was intended to describe her, as well as the tree.

She hugged him, her face tipped up towards his. Unbearably beautiful. 'Thank you so much, Joe.'

He couldn't think of anything in this world that he needed to do right now other than kiss her. There was nothing else...

The clock on the mantelpiece chimed. Ten o'clock.

'Maisie will be calling soon.' He broke free, and walked over to the table, stacking the empty cartons back into the box.

'Yes, I suppose... How did you know?'

He knew, because he'd called Maisie and let her know that Neve hadn't gone down to London as expected. He'd planned today like a military operation—the surprise left on her doorstep, the friends who would invite her to lunch. The one thing he hadn't planned on was being a part of all that.

'I...um...spoke to Maisie yesterday.'

She stared at him. Keeping anything from those canny blue eyes was nigh on impossible. 'Then you're coming too.'

'Maisie mentioned it. I wasn't going to but...' Things were different, now. 'Yeah, I'm coming too. I'll have to pop back home to feed Almond afterwards, though.'

She nodded. 'We can go to your place before we go. Pick Almond up and bring her here with some food and her basket. She'll be fine. The stove keeps the kitchen warm.'

One more step. One more thing that twined their lives together. 'So you're holding my cat hostage, are you? To make sure I'll come back here after lunch.'

She grinned. 'Yeah. Pay up or the cat gets it.'

'Get's what?'

'Don't you know an empty threat when you hear it?'

Joe shook his head. She was delightful, irrepressible, and more joyful than he'd ever seen her. He could deny her nothing.

'You have a problem with that?' Her eyes were questioning.

'No. No problem.'

It was dark by the time Joe drew up in front of Neve's house. They'd had a great time at Maisie's. There had been sixteen around her table, and although it had been a little crowded the good cheer had made a virtue of that. Joe had seemed more relaxed than Neve had ever seen him.

Almond raised her head sleepily when Neve opened the kitchen door, and padded up to Joe, nuzzling at his legs until he picked her up and stroked her. Glancing at the baubles from the lower limbs of the tree, which were now scattered across the floor, he grinned. 'What have you been up to, then? You're in big trouble…'

Almond looked up at him and gave a meow, almost as if she was answering the question.

'Okay. So if you didn't do it, who did?' Joe raised one eyebrow and Almond ignored him, settling onto his chest and starting to purr.

'Hey! She said she didn't do it.' Neve grinned at him.

'Oh, so you're on her side, are you?' Joe set Almond back on her feet and went to gather up the baubles from the floor. Almond trotted after him, trying to bat the sparkling playthings out of his reach.

Neve couldn't help but laugh. Joe didn't compromise for anyone, but the tiny creature had him wound around her little finger. Neve picked up the empty food bowl and tore open one of the packets of cat food that lay on the counter.

Almond galloped across the room as if she hadn't been fed in months, nuzzling at Neve's legs and purring. Joe straightened up from replacing the decorations on the tree and chuckled. 'That's right. Show a guy where your heart really lies.'

Today had been such a lovely day. The thought that he

might still take Almond and go home tonight was…unthinkable. 'Would you like something to eat?'

He grinned, throwing himself down on the sofa. So far so good. 'Food is the one thing I don't want right now. I don't think I'll be eating again for another week.'

Neve flipped open one of the kitchen cupboards and retrieved the emergency brandy from behind the biscuit tin. Collected a couple of glasses and walked over to the sofa, sitting down next to him.

'You can have a drink, though?'

He'd waved away offers of wine with his lunch and passed on the after-dinner port because he was driving. Perhaps he could be persuaded not to do any more driving today. Diffidently, Neve held out one of the glasses.

'I really shouldn't.'

'Joe, I know we said we were going to take this slowly. And I appreciate that, I really do. But there's nothing to say we can't take it slowly together, is there? I want you to stay here, and the sofa bed's comfortable enough…'

Maybe she'd gone too far. Maybe she was going to spoil everything. She shrank back from him.

'Hey…hey, don't do that.' He reached out for her, catching her hand. 'We said we'd be honest with each other, and that means asking for what we want. I thought you might want me to go, to give you a little time to think things over, that's all… I guess I should stop trying to second-guess you, eh?'

'Shall we try that one again?'

'Yeah, I think so.'

Neve sat down next to him. 'I'd like you to stay tonight. We could think things over together.'

He grinned. 'I'd like that, too.'

'So…' She proffered the glass again. 'Would you like a brandy?'

'Love one.'

* * *

She and Joe had talked until well past midnight, curled up on the sofa together. Stories about his time in the army, about her training down in London. His childhood in Canada, the trips up to the cabin in the north, when his grandfather had taught Joe and his brothers how to fish and his grandmother had told them the Inupiat stories that every boy should take careful note of before he reached manhood.

Finally, Joe brushed a kiss on her forehead, tipping her gently out of his arms. 'We really should get some sleep. It's been a long day.'

'Can't I hold you? Just a little longer.'

He grinned. 'Yeah. As long as you like.'

Downstairs, with the smell of the Christmas tree and the sparkling lights, seemed the right place. Joe pulled the sofa bed open and Neve fetched a duvet and some blankets to keep them warm. She went upstairs to change into her pyjamas, and found Joe under the duvet when she returned.

'Right here.' He patted the space next to him, and she lay down.

'Comfortable?'

'Yes.' She was lying on her back, staring at the ceiling. This wasn't quite what she'd had in mind.

'Hmm.' Joe seemed to be engaged in a complex rearrangement of the bedclothes. Blankets were pulled this way and the duvet pushed that. Then he gently rolled her onto her side, wrapping the duvet around her and pulling her into a soft layer of down between his body and hers. One arm wound around her waist, held her tight and firm against the shapeless, reassuring bulk of his body. 'Is that okay?'

'That's nice.' She stared into the darkness for a moment. 'The lease on your cottage. You said you'd given it up.'

'I'll call the agent when the office reopens and say that

I've changed my mind. I doubt that they'll have re-let it at this time of the year.'

'I...don't want...'

'Are you going to chicken out on me now? I was going to go because of you. And now I'm staying for you. I can't promise to stay for good, but I will promise to see this through.' She felt his chest rise and fall. 'Canada will wait for me. Maybe I'll get to show it to you one day.'

'Maybe you will. I think I'd like that.'

'Yeah. I'd like it too.' His hand found hers and held it loosely. 'It's late. Want a bedtime story?'

'One of your gran's?' Neve doubted whether she'd be able to sleep like this, but she didn't want to move.

'Of course. The one about the boy who went fishing...'

The story turned out to be a long one, and Neve never did get to hear the moral of the tale. Before he'd finished she was fast asleep.

CHAPTER EIGHTEEN

'OH, NO!' THE SOFA bed rocked alarmingly, propelling Neve into grudging wakefulness. A startled yowl as Almond decided that getting out of the way was probably the best course of action, and Joe's running footsteps.

'What?' Neve pulled the duvet over her head. If the house was on fire, perhaps he'd put it out without any need for intervention on her part.

'We're late.'

'What for?' She opened one eye. Joe had his back to her and was pulling on his jeans. 'It's Boxing Day. What's so important?'

He turned. Three-sixty-degree view. Nice.

'It's the Boxing Day soccer match. Starts at eleven.'

'It's a Boxing Day *football* match. And it's only nine o'clock.'

'We need to be there early to help clear the snow off the pitch. And I've got to get back home to pick up my kit then back here to pick you up.'

'You're playing?'

He gave her a broad grin. Neve would walk a hundred miles in the snow for that grin. In her pyjamas. 'You want to be my girl? Then you've got to watch me play soccer.' He bent to grab his boots. 'I'll be back to get you in half an hour.'

* * *

It turned out that hard work in the freezing air was just what she needed and the traditional Leminster vs Cryersbridge Boxing Day football match afforded plenty of both. Muffled in coats and scarves, the whole community turned up at the local school, which had opened its changing rooms for the occasion, and was helping clear the snow from the pitch that the tractor had missed.

Joe disappeared with the rest of the team to get changed. The local Guides were out, doing a roaring trade in hot drinks, and the teams decided that taking off their sweatpants and shirts would be a little beyond the call of duty. With their team shirts covered up, it wasn't too easy to tell who was on which side, but everyone seemed disposed to cheer both sides anyway, just for turning out in the subzero temperatures.

'I still reckon you could have taken that shot…' Both teams and most of the spectators had made a beeline for The Bleeding Hart, which had opened its doors in honour of the occasion, as soon as the final whistle had sounded.

'Everyone's an expert.' Joe grinned down at her.

'Just taking an interest. And that goal was yours for the taking.'

He shrugged amiably. 'Adrian was in a better position.'

And Joe was the stronger player. Adrian was only sixteen and the youngest member of the team. No one had expected him to score and when he had, he'd run the whole length of the pitch, arms outstretched in an impromptu victory dance, while everyone on the touchline had cheered. Neve supposed that that was what Joe had intended all along.

'You took a bit of a tumble in the first half. Are you all right?'

'Yeah, fine.' He displayed a length of sticking plaster

wrapped around his wrist. 'I think our beloved team coach overdid the strapping a bit. It's just a graze.'

'Did he clean it?'

Joe rolled his eyes. 'No, we thought we'd see whether we could set up a culture so we left all the dirt in there.'

'Right. Just as long as I know.' Neve caught hold of the front of his jacket, looking up into his face. 'Not going to add to your collection of scars, is it?'

His arm around her waist, he pulled her close. 'If it does, I'll have something to remember you by.'

'Me? It wasn't me who tackled you.'

'Yours was the face that flashed in front of my eyes when I hit the ground.' His lips were about an inch from her ear.

'You didn't go down that hard. And if you were hallucinating, you should have come off the pitch.' She was tingling with pleasure. Joe seemed so… He wasn't different. Just more the man he ought to be.

It looked as if the party wasn't going to break up any time soon. But Joe downed a half-pint of beer with astonishing alacrity, was slapped on the back by his teammates and stopped to congratulate Adrian on the winning goal. Then he was back at her side.

'Ready to go?'

Neve had reckoned on being here a while and had been pacing herself, sipping her orange juice slowly. She downed the remainder of the glass in one go. 'Yes. I'm ready.'

He grinned. 'Let's go, then.'

Outside, in the car park, she caught his hand. 'Do you think you could…?'

'What?'

'I want you to kiss me.'

One look at his face told Neve that was exactly what he wanted too. Winding his arms around her waist, he brushed a gentle kiss against her lips.

'Not like that, you idiot.'

'Like this?' His kiss was warm and giving. Crushing her against him, he almost lifted her off her feet.

'Much better.' Neve looked around as a wolf-whistle sounded behind her. One of the Leminster team waved at them cheerily and disappeared through the doors of the pub.

'How long do you think it'll be before Maisie hears about this?' His grin was intoxicating.

'I reckon…' Neve checked her watch '…about six o'clock. It's got a fair way to go.'

'You did this on purpose, didn't you?'

'Do you mind?'

'Mind?' He dropped another kiss onto her lips. 'I was thinking about taking you back inside and doing this all over again. That way everyone'll notice.'

'Nah. Once is enough to start the rumour. You can take me home and do it again.'

Joe attacked the snow-filled roads with unusual reck-lessness, even spinning the wheels once or twice. No need to ask what all the hurry was about.

They shed their coats on the way to the kitchen. When they got there, Joe lifted her up onto the table, pulling her boots off. Then, suddenly, he straightened up. 'We said that we'd wait yesterday…'

'A lot can happen in a day.'

'Yes, but…' He was looking at her intently. 'I won't rush you into anything, Neve. This is much too impor-tant to me.'

She put her finger over his lips. 'I know what I want, Joe. Just promise me that you won't lie to me. Not about anything.'

'You already have that promise. I'll make it again…'

No need. She pulled him towards her, kissing him, revelling in the softness of his lips. 'I don't want to wait any longer, Joe.'

'Good.' He hugged her tight. 'Because you've been driving me crazy...'

'How crazy?'

He chuckled. 'That's going to take some time to answer.'

By the time they made it to the bedroom she'd already stripped off his sweater and shirt, his skin warm against her cheek as he carried her up the stairs. He laid her on the bed and she pulled him down next to her.

His dark gaze found hers. 'There's something I want to ask you.'

'Anything you want, Joe...'

He shook his head. 'Don't say that until you've heard what it is. You might not like it.'

'Then I'll say so. That's the whole point of trust, isn't it?'

He nodded, kissing her. 'Don't take this the wrong way, Neve, but I want to be the one that you rely on and who cares for you. I don't want to tell you what to think or what to do but...'

She put her finger to his lips, silencing him. 'I know. I want that too.'

That sudden grin of his. He didn't need to break through the barriers she'd shielded herself with, Joe's smile made her want to rip them down herself with her bare hands.

Slowly. Slowly. He stripped her naked then pulled off his own jeans. They traded caresses, taking their time over each one. Each touch of his fingers on her skin felt like a bright, new beginning.

'Look at me, Neve.'

The unbearable intimacy of looking straight into his eyes while he made love to her. Knowing that he was watching her, too. Joe rolled her onto her back, settling his hips between her legs. Slid slowly inside her, his gaze never leaving hers.

'I see you, Joe.'

'And I see you. Can you do this?' The connection between them was almost tangible. Frightening in its intensity.

'Yes.'

He took her hand in his, guiding her arm up over her head, and wrapping her fingers around one of the brass rails of the bedstead. Then the other. The feeling of being stretched out beneath him was glorious, and Neve hung on tight as he started to move.

She could see her own pleasure reflected in his face. He was reading her like a book, finding infinite variations of each caress, long and slow, or hard and demanding. Breaking her in his embrace. Making her strong.

They came together. By this time one powerful movement from him was all it took to plunge them both into a release that should have blocked out everything else. But he was there still, with her. Joe. From this moment on, it would only be Joe.

She was clinging to him. All he wanted to do was to please her, keep her safe. Keep her here, with him. Suddenly *safe* and *with him* didn't seem like so much of a contradiction in terms.

'Okay, honey?' He smoothed a strand of golden hair from her forehead.

'Joe…' Her fingers were digging uncomfortably into the flesh of his arms but he didn't care. Just wanted her to hang on tight to him. 'What did you do?'

She was there with him, in that warm, after-sex place where there was no thought. No consideration of what you were going to say before you opened your mouth. No tact and no caution, just the unvarnished, beautiful truth.

'I...' What the hell *had* he done? The unthinkable was jangling insistently in his head, demanding to be heard. 'I just loved you, sweetheart.'

It was more than that, and they both knew it. She'd given herself up to him. He wondered if, now that the moment had passed, she'd try to deny it.

'Hmm. You're a thief, Joe Lamont. You've stolen my heart.'

'Thieves don't generally give you their own in return.' He rolled her over, pulling her with him, letting her sprawl across his chest. Soft, pale skin with a delicious flush of pink. He ran his fingers slowly down her spine, counting each vertebral disc.

'Same number as yours.' She snuggled against him. Joe could get seriously used to this.

'Just checking.'

She chuckled, her lips forming a little air-kiss, as if she wasn't quite done with kissing yet, but his lips were too far away. 'You can do a thorough inventory. In a while.' She stretched across his chest.

'Take as long as you like.' If she thought that she was going to get out of this bed any time soon, she was wrong. He knew now that he had the power to keep her here, and he was shamelessly unafraid to use it.

She grinned. Reached lazily for his hand and pulled it to her lips. 'You have great hands. You know that?'

They were her faithful, dedicated servants, ready to do whatever she wanted. 'I love you, Neve.'

She raised her head, focussing on his face. 'You do?'

'Afraid so.' He wondered whether she'd say it back. Whether he deserved her love. And then she said it, and his heart practically burst from his chest.

'I love you too, Joe.'

CHAPTER NINETEEN

THE LAST FIVE MONTHS had been…pretty much every emotion that Neve could imagine. It had taken time, some professional help and a lot of love before Joe had been able to tell her everything, and when he had the nightmares had returned with a vengeance. But he'd stuck with it, showing a stubborn courage that wrung her heart. She'd shared those dark nights with him and as he'd healed his passion for medicine had returned.

He told her that he loved her every day. Proved it, with a constancy that was impossible to doubt. Neve had feared repeating the patterns of the past with Joe, but he had shown her a different future.

Now it was time to celebrate. Joe had completed his six-week clinical attachment at the hospital with flying colours and was now eligible to apply for a job in the NHS. His parents and youngest brother had flown over from Canada for a holiday, and Joe and Neve were spending a week with them in London. There would be seven for dinner tonight, as Neve's parents were joining them.

'You look stunning.' Joe had booked them into a nice hotel as a treat, and was lounging in an easy chair, watching her get dressed.

'You like my dress?' Neve twirled around to give him the full effect.

'The dress is great. *You* are stunning.'

Joe had a way with a compliment. She walked across to him, standing between his outstretched legs. 'So I wasted all that time I spent choosing it?'

'No. If you hadn't spent all morning on it, I'd be inclined to rip it off your back and make love to you.' He grinned. 'Again.'

'But you know that if you tore one stitch of this, you'd been in deep trouble.'

'Exactly. So we'll be on time for dinner.'

Neve chuckled, perching herself on his knee. 'Well, you're looking particularly handsome tonight, too.' He was wearing a crisp white shirt, still open at the neck, and dark trousers. The matching jacket was slung over the back of the chair.

'Thank you. I have a particular reason…'

'What, because of the parents? My mum and dad think you're wonderful already, and your parents don't seem all that stuck on formality.' Neve had only met Joe's parents the day before, but she felt she already knew them well from long conversations via the internet.

'No. There's something else. Two things, in fact. The first is that I have a job.'

'Another one? What is it this time?' Joe seemed to be in constant demand, helping with various projects in the village. On a couple of occasions Neve had worried that he'd taken on too much, but Joe always would thrive on a challenge.

'Guess.' His eyes were gleaming with suppressed excitement.

'I can see it's something a bit special.'

'Yes. Something very special…'

'Something…' Neve hardly dared to ask. She knew how much this meant to Joe. 'Something to do with medicine?'

'You're getting warm.'

'At the hospital?'

'Warmer.'

'Ow! Tell me, Joe, I can't bear it.'

'When I was doing my clinical attachment, a post in surgery came up. It's pretty senior, but I asked if I could apply anyway, and they said they'd welcome it. I got an email with a formal offer this afternoon.'

'Joe!' Neve leaned forward and kissed him. 'Why didn't you say something?'

'Because I wanted this moment.'

She dug her fingers into his ribs. 'I'm going to get you back for this, Joe Lamont. You wait and see, I'm going to find something to surprise *you* with and make you as happy as I am right now...'

'You surprise me every day, honey.' He kissed her and she melted into his arms. 'Do you think your father will be pleased?'

'I expect so. What's he got to do with it?'

'I wouldn't want him to think that his daughter's associating with a guy with no prospects...'

'He doesn't. He's a very good judge of character.'

'Good. Because I told you there were *two* things...' He shifted her gently off his knee and got to his feet. 'Come here.'

Joe took her hand and led her over to the high French windows, which opened onto a stone balcony. Below them were the gardens at the back of the hotel, where they'd taken tea that afternoon.

'What are you doing? You've got an air of mystery about you.'

'Really?'

Neve slid her arms around his waist. 'Don't give me that innocent look. Now I know there's something going on.'

'Yeah, okay. There's something going on.'

He reached behind him, unclasping her fingers, and

suddenly he dropped to one knee. Neve's hand flew to her mouth. It couldn't be… 'Joe. What is this?'

'Marry me.'

A tear ran down her cheek and she brushed it away. It was typical of Joe, no long speeches or declarations. Everything else had already been talked about, they knew each other's dreams, and these two words sealed his promise to fulfil them.

'Yes.'

'I'll be a good husband and a good father.'

'I know.'

'I'll love you always…'

'Yes! Do you hear me?'

He grinned, and her poor heart flipped another somersault. If he kept going like this, she was going to die of happiness. 'Yeah, I heard you. Just wanted you to say it again.'

'Yes.' She bent down and kissed him. 'Yes. I'll cook your dinner…'

'I'd prefer it if we took turns.'

'Wash your clothes…'

'We have a washing machine.'

'Warm your bed…'

'Yeah. That I'm going to insist on.'

'Make babies with you.'

'Now you're talking. Give me your hand.' He rolled his eyes. 'No, not that one.' He reached for her left hand.

'You've got a ring?' Neve could have jumped for joy. Would have done if she hadn't been wearing such high heels.

'I've got a ring.' He felt in his pocket and something sparkled in his hand. 'Now, it was far too good the first time not to repeat. Let's take it from the top. Will you marry me?'

'Yes, Joe. I want to tell you *yes* for every day of my life. Starting now.'

He bent to kiss her hand then slipped the ring onto her finger. Neve stared at it.

'Say something…' A note of uncertainty sounded in his voice.

'I love it. I love you. I'm so happy…' She pulled him to his feet and kissed him.

'Me too. You're everything to me, Neve.'

A loud swoosh from below, and then a bang, and the sky was suddenly full of coloured stars.

'Must be a celebration.' Her gaze didn't leave his face.

'Yeah. My kid brother's down there with a couple of the hotel staff.'

Another two rockets shot up into the air, exploding into the night sky.

'He knew about this?'

Joe kissed her again. Long and loving and warm. 'All I told him was that he was to set off the rockets when he saw me kiss you.'

All she could see was Joe. All she knew was his kiss. 'Seems like he's missed his cue. The only fireworks I can see are up here.'

Joe chuckled. 'Perhaps we should give him a break and just keep going until he gets it right.' He kissed her again. Stars exploded into the sky, and the world lurched under her feet.

Neve wrapped her arms around his neck. 'Yes. Let's just keep going…'

* * * * *

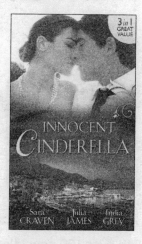

MILLS & BOON®

Exciting new titles
coming next month

With over 100 new titles available every month,
find out what exciting romances
lie ahead next month.

Visit
www.millsandboon.co.uk/comingsoon
to find out more!